State of Fear

Collapse Series #8

D1280165

Summer Lane

1

For Scott.

Marrying you will be the greatest adventure.

Here's to October 1st.

Prologue

"It's okay, everybody made it out alive," Chris said.

He reached across the seat and held my hand. I grasped his fingers firmly in mine. We drove in a roaring, screeching Humvee out of San Francisco, the city ablaze in our wake. The utter destruction was behind us, and the barren desert was before us.

I could feel Uriah's steely gaze on the back of my head as we drove, and as my fingers held Chris's hand, I could feel the cold tension in Chris's arm, the controlled fury behind his eyes. He was angry about San Francisco; he was angry at me.

Truth be told, I was angry at him, too.

After I had escaped the devastation of an assassination mission into the Omega stronghold, Red Grove, I had expected Chris to be a little more...overjoyed about my survival. I had evaded death yet again. I felt like Chris had erected a wall around his heart, afraid – once again – to love me, because he thought I had died.

But really, we were all going to die.

It was just a matter of when.

Chapter One

Sector 27 – Somewhere in the California Desert, Death Valley

"What's wrong with you, Cassidy?" Chris demands.

I have never seen him so angry with me. Not like this.

"I have to go," I say.

My words are hollow, expressionless.

"This is about me, isn't it?" Chris retorts, eyes flashing. He stands up from the couch, his hands curled into fists, his knuckles turning white. "You're angry with me. You're angry, so you're leaving. Where is this coming from? This isn't like you! You don't leave, Cassie. You stand and fight. You get the job done."

"I know," I reply, arms folded across my chest. "That's why I have to leave. I won't get anything done here. Not anymore."

"That's a lie."

"It's not. And you know it." I turn my head, slowly meeting his gaze. "I am not some innocent flower child, Chris. I'm not just some girl anymore. I'm a soldier, I've killed a lot of people, and I've seen a lot of the people I love die. I can't get away from that – ever. Not here. These people...the militias. They're great, really. But they don't get it. They don't get *me*. I scare them. I need to go. I need to start over."

"You *need* to stay here."

I sigh. I am sure of so few things in this moment.

I am sure that I want Omega destroyed. I am sure that I miss my father, and my friends, and my old life. I am sure that I love Chris, too. Those things will never change, ever.

But I am unsure of what we should do next, now that Omega has ravaged our coastline and nuked our cities.

I am tired. I am a dry, withered vine in need of a long, soothing rain.

I feel myself drifting away from Chris, away from the militias. Away from the same fight, over and over again. I want real security and safety. Real warmth and victory.

California is the enemy's now.

I don't want to be here, not anymore. There is too much death. Too much blood.

"Come with me," I say.

"You know I can't do that."

"And why not? Why can't we all just relocate?"

"Because we are all that is standing between Omega and their total domination of the West Coast!"

"Chris, they're already here. We need to get out of here and regroup, or what's left of our forces is going to be obliterated."

"No. I don't believe that."

"Always the optimist," I whisper. "Maybe you're right. But I can't stay here. You have to let me go. You know my time is up here."

Chris stares at me, electric green eyes wide and shocked.

A thick quietness hangs in the room.

"What will happen to us?" Chris asks softly.

Not him, not me. But both of us. Together. Bound by something deeper and stronger than mere attraction.

"We'll survive," I tell him. "We always do."

Chris's face is tight, contained. I swear I can hear him screaming on the inside.

"I always thought we would find a way to stay together," Chris says at last, his voice tense. "Even in the middle of all this...insanity."

"This isn't forever," I say. "You can come join me when your work here is done."

"My work isn't done until Omega is eradicated from this state."

We both know what that means: either Omega loses or Chris dies trying. Period.

"I will always love you, Cassidy Hart," Chris says. Crystalline tears shine in the corners of his eyes.

"And I will always love you," I reply. "This doesn't change that."

This time, I cannot keep the tremor out of my voice.

I stand, ever so slowly, and Chris places his hand on my hip. He is close enough that I can smell him – the scent of warm coffee mingled with gunpowder and fresh dirt. We look at each other, worn, beaten, tired, spent. There is so much love between us, so much loyalty. Chris leans forward, his breath hot against my cheek, pressing his lips against my face. I close my eyes, the familiar touch of his kiss so comforting, yet so heartbreaking. His lips find their way to mine, and he pulls me close in a strong embrace. I kiss him like I have never kissed him before, like a drowning woman desperate for air. I thread my fingers through his hair and grasp tightly. I feel the hot, acidic sting of salty tears washing down my cheeks. We kiss until we have no more breath, until Chris pulls away, wipes the tears off my cheeks with his thumb, and we separate. Two separate continents adrift in the sea, once again torn apart by war.

He says nothing. I say nothing.

He takes his jacket, he turns, he opens the door.

"This isn't the end," he says quietly. "We will win this."

He leaves.

And I am alone again. Truly alone.

***

Sector 27 is the most barren stretch of wilderness I've ever seen. From my vantage point beneath the camouflaged loading dock in the side of a rocky mountain, I can see for miles in every direction. Nothing but desert hills and plains. It's beautiful, really. The colors, the landscapes, the rise and fall of the earth.

So different than what I am used to.

But barren. Empty, like an alien planet.

I close my eyes, and I think of San Francisco, the Golden Gate Bridge cascading into the harbor. I think of Veronica Klaus – the Omega Chancellor – and her smug, calculating smile. I think of the destruction of the city and the ravaged ruins of Alcatraz Island.

Gone. All of it.

Finally, Omega has pushed us out of the way, and they now rule the California coastline with an iron fist.

"Cassidy, are you okay?"

Elle Costas approaches me from the shadows. Her short, black hair frames a pale face and bright, blue eyes. Her dog, a German Shepherd explosives detection canine named Bravo, follows closely.

"Yeah, sure," I reply, forcing a smile. "You?"

"Mmm," she says. "I know when you're lying."

"Do you?"

"Yeah. You're not okay."

I fold my arms across my chest.

"Well, none of us are, really," I reply.

Elle is barely sixteen years old, but she has the maturity of someone far older. I don't bother hiding things from her. She is too smart for that...and so is her dog.

"Are you really going to leave California?" she asks quietly.

I don't answer right away. Here, in the bowels of Sector 27, it is easy to believe that the invasion of the

West Coast never happened. The eight-thousand-man force of the militias and National Guard are living beneath this mountain, licking their wounds and planning their next move.

"Yes," I say at last. "I think it's time."

Elle places her hand on top of Bravo's head.

"So you're going to Alaska, then?"

"Yeah."

A long silence hangs between us.

"I want to come with you," she says.

"Are you sure?"

"Yes. My family's dead. I might as well."

"What about your Uncle Manny and Aunt Arlene?"

Elle sighs.

"I love them," she tells me, "but I hate it here. I came to Sector 27 once, did I tell you that, Commander?" She looks sad. "Bravo and I...we left friends here. Jay, Georgia and Flash were their names."

"What happened to them?" I ask.

"I don't know. I thought I would see them when we came here...but they're gone." She shrugs. "I want to come with you. Please, Commander. Don't say no."

I place my hand on Elle's shoulder.

"Of course I'm not going to say that... You can come."

She smiles.

"Thank you."

The sun begins to rise over the hills, spreading a pinkish light across the desert. The light is quickly swallowed up by dark, black clouds. It starts raining.

"Commander Young is staying here, isn't he?" Elle asks, frowning.

A dagger of pain pierces my heart.

"Yes," I say. "He's staying."

"Will he meet us in Alaska, then?"

"I don't know. Maybe."

Elle furrows her brow.

"He still loves you, doesn't he?"

I look at her sharply.

"Elle, I don't want to talk about this, okay?" I clear my throat. "We have to go meet with Arlene."

I check my analog watch. Yes. It's time.

Besides, I can't just stand around staring at the sunrise. It makes me think about what I am about to do – and what Chris is about to do, too.

We walk through Sector 27's loading docks, past dozens of parked Humvees and pickups. We enter the stairwell and climb one flight below, where the concrete hallways are tall and ominous. We pass the chow hall – which is noisy and full of hungry soldiers – and a section of barracks for female militia fighters.

In the hours after arriving here, Chris and I had dragged ourselves to our respective barracks, collapsing with exhaustion. When I awoke, I couldn't remember where I was. It took a few minutes for me to gain my bearings...and then it all came back to me in a tidal wave. I had sat up, winded, and wincing. I had been punctured by shrapnel during my mission to Red Grove and had never asked the medical team to treat it.

I remember looking down at it, surprised to find that the wound had reopened. Blood had pooled on my cot and soaked into my clothes.

Oops.

So I ended up spending all morning in the medical wing, getting sanitized and stitched up, receiving a new uniform and taking a hot shower...right after Chris stormed into my private quarters, demanding to know what I was thinking about Alaska. How could I leave California? How could I leave *him*?

It's only temporary, I think. *It will be okay.*

We reach the last room on the right. I open the metal doors. It is huge inside, a long, dark room with a massive table. Seated around the table are Arlene and Manny Costas, Chris Young, Vera Wright, Andrew Decker, and someone who I have not seen in a long time: Devin, from Monterey.

Manny and Arlene are sitting far apart. Manny's wild, gray hair is tucked under a red bandana, and his usually cheery face is imprinted with a deep frown. Chris stares at me as I walk in, a deep, fiery gaze that burns a hole through my chest.

"Commander Hart," Devin says, flashing his pearly whites.

He is a Navy SEAL, just like Chris. I am surprised to see him here.

"Devin," I say. "Good to see you."

There are several other militia and National Guard commanders sitting around the table, too. I do not recognize them. They are leaders that have been stationed in Sector 27 since the beginning of the invasion.

"Well, we're all here," Arlene says, smoothing her white hair away from her face. She looks worn and weary. "Let's begin."

Vera locks eyes with me as I take a seat with Elle. Her blond hair is slicked back into a tight ponytail. Andrew is sitting beside her, holding her hand under the table.

"I think the first order of business," I say, looking at Arlene, "is to explain to everybody in this room why the safe haven in Alaska was never previously mentioned."

Arlene stands up, slowly making her way to the front of the room. She waves to the back of the room, and the lights dim. A bright projector tosses a glowing image of an Alaskan map on the wall.

"Secrecy was of the utmost importance," Arlene replies, avoiding my eyes.

"Oh, you mean the kind of secrecy that you guys had in Sky City?" Vera snorts. "Because that worked out great for everyone, right?"

Silence.

Manny's frown deepens.

"This is much different," Arlene goes on, clearing her throat. I notice that her fingers are trembling slightly. "This is not a military camp. This is a survivor colony. There are thousands of people here. They have a working government – an elected president, a small senate…everything."

"How do we benefit in any way by leaving California to the wolves and high-tailing it up to the middle of nowhere?" Manny suddenly asks, tapping his long fingers on the table. "Hmm? We'll just be trading surviving in the desert for surviving in the snow, wrestling with moose and whatever else Mother Nature decides to throw at us."

"Well, first of all," Arlene says, "we'll be free from radiation fallout. Thousands of miles away, lots of fresh air. It will be safe enough to go outside without being covered or wearing gas masks. And second of all, we could regroup, reorganize and strategize against Omega."

"I've heard that before," Andrew mutters.

Vera glances at him, her lips pursed.

"Okay, but I've got a question," she says, raising her hand. "Omega is here now, in California. They've finally got their stronghold on the West Coast. We've lost that battle. Why not just sacrifice the state and pull back somewhere closer – like Nevada, or Texas?"

"Because we're not entirely sure what's there," Chris replies.

His voice is strong and slightly raspy. He is tired.

I don't look at him. I can't.

"Plus, the nuclear fallout is being carried east, anyway," Arlene continues. "Alaska will give us a chance to be so far away from the invasion that we can actually rest easy, knowing that Omega troops or patrols won't be creeping up on us at night."

I stare at my hands.

Arlene's words make sense, but I know, deep down, that no matter where we go, we will never be completely free of Omega. They will find us, eventually.

"I'm going," I say, placing my palms on the table. "We've lost this battle. It's time to think outside the box. Omega is too powerful. We've got eight thousand men – that's *it*! Omega's got millions of foot soldiers, and their forces in San Francisco alone almost obliterated us. We've got to be smarter than just forming a blockade against them." I shake my head. "We need more reinforcements, and we need to get out of here. Because they will come, and this time they will be too powerful, and we *will* die."

My words hang in the air like a poisonous cloud.

"We need to base our operations outside of the state, somewhere where we can safely disappear," I go on. "Remember back in the early days of the war, when we would fight during the night and disappear into the mountains during the day? We can't do that anymore, not in California. Our advantage is gone – Omega's got the upper hand. We have to gain an advantage again, and I don't see how we can do that unless we make a full retreat to Alaska."

Vera stands up.

"Cassidy's right!" she says, glaring at everyone. "We've been fighting in the same stupid skirmishes over and over again, and I'm freaking sick of it. I'm sick of watching my friends and family die. It's time for a change. I'm going to Alaska, too. Count me in."

Andrew looks shocked, paling a little.

"I'm going, too," Elle says. "Me and Bravo, I mean."

Arlene stares at her.

"Elle, you don't –"

"Don't try to stop me," Elle interrupts. There is an edge to her voice.

"I'm going if you're going," Manny says, raising an eyebrow. "You're not going to be wrestling any moose without me."

Elle smiles faintly.

19

"Manny!" Arlene exclaims. "You don't mean that."

Manny says nothing. I see a spark of anger in his eyes – and hurt. I know he is angry with Arlene. His wife has kept secrets from him for too long – secrets about Sky City, secrets about nuclear warheads at the disposal of the militias, and now secrets about a safe colony in Alaska.

He is done. He is as frustrated as I am.

I look around the room. A few of the commanders raise their hands, announcing their decision to relocate to Alaska, as well. The drama unfolds before my eyes, and I realize something...we are breaking up. Our little militia, our group of leaders.

Our coalition is not growing...it's falling apart.

That knowledge scares me, but somehow I realize that it is a necessary evolution.

I am done with this madness.

"And what about the eight thousand men who are living in this base?" Chris asks angrily. "Do they get a choice in this?"

"We'll present the information to the entire militia," I say firmly. "And they can decide what they want to do. If they want to remain here under your command, or if they want to relocate to Alaska."

Chris's green eyes flicker.

"And what if they all decide to stay here, Commander Hart?" he asks.

"Then I guess I'll be going to Alaska by myself."

My words are sharp, and I look away from Chris. I slide my hands off the table and fold them on my lap. I don't want anyone to see how badly they are shaking.

Arlene is standing at the head of the table, seemingly shocked into silence by Manny and Elle's declaration of departure. After several long minutes, the conversation dies down, and there is quiet once again.

"Tell us where it is," I command Arlene. "Tell us everything you know."

***

The survivor colony in Alaska is called Yukon City. It is located on a secluded peninsula called Whittier, a place bathed in fog and rain, based on the pictures that Arlene is flipping through in her slideshow.

"The colony is mostly comprised of refugees, but there is a fairly powerful para-military presence there to protect it," Arlene says. "The city itself is almost like an island. It's surrounded by mountains on all sides, and flanked by the ocean. The only way to access it is to take a ferry from the mainland, or to fly in." She absently brushes back her wispy gray hair. She continues, "During World War Two, the United States established a secret military defense base there: Camp Sullivan. It was small, but it was well-hidden. Whittier itself still *is* well hidden, as a matter of fact, which is why the colony was established there."

"Sounds secluded," Chris remarks. "Population?"

"Several thousand. Many survivors who fled the big Alaskan cities like Anchorage or Juneau came here. There is a two-and-a-half-mile tunnel that cuts through the mountains – the only way to reach Whittier from the rest of the state. In fact, it's the longest highway tunnel in the world. It's heavily guarded by militia units and the Alaskan National Guard."

"What's the leadership like in Whittier?" Vera says.

"They have an elected president, as well as a senate."

"Who is the president?" I ask.

"A woman named Mauve Bacardi," Arlene replies. "She was a senator for Alaska before the Collapse. The people naturally gravitated toward electing her – she has a way with words, and the survivors love her."

"Can she be trusted?" Manny asks.

Arlene doesn't look at him as she answers, "I should hope so."

Chris never removes his gaze from the projected images on the wall, his back tense and straight, his shoulders squared.

"Yukon City is the biggest survivor colony that we know of," Arlene goes on. "Intel for the militias has suggested that there are thousands of different colonies around the country, but the Alaskan camp is the largest – as well as the safest. Mostly because of the nuclear fallout – people want to be safe. They want to breathe fresh air, and people have been flocking to Whittier ever since Omega dropped the first nuclear bomb."

Elle strokes Bravo's head, smiling wistfully.

I wonder if she is thinking what I am thinking:

How nice would it be to walk outside and not be afraid of the air?

"What about the Pacific Northwest Alliance?" Chris says suddenly. "Have they played a part in this survivor's colony?"

"They have," Arlene confirms. "Commander Young, there is much information about the surviving members of this Collapse, and most of it is shrouded in secrecy, if only to protect the information from leaking to traitors in our own ranks."

Somehow, this cools the embers of my anger a bit.

We have had many traitors infiltrate our ranks. Perhaps keeping this information really *was* the wisest decision Arlene and her peers made. Perhaps it has protected Yukon City all of this time.

"How do you stay in contact with the colony?" I ask.

"We don't," Arlene says. "We protect Yukon by cutting them off, to put it simply. Their location and existence is untraceable to the enemy. We would only communicate with them directly in a matter of dire circumstances."

I bite my lip.

By going to Yukon City I will be completely cut off from California. From Chris.

Is this what I really want to do?

Yes. We need this.

"Yukon City has many secrets," Arlene goes on, turning to face the room. "I can't reveal all of them here....President Bacardi will enlighten you once you arrive. However, you should know that by going to Alaska, you will not be there to rest and relax. You will be there to search for additional recruits or weaponry that can aid in our fight against Omega. You know that we are in desperate need of both."

"How will they know we're coming if we have no communication with them?" Vera asks, rolling her eyes. "Hello. That's stupid."

"One of our aircraft will drop a message to alert them that you are on your way," Arlene explains. "You'll be dropped just on the other side of the mountains – and you'll take a convoy through the tunnel to reach Whittier."

"Who's the commanding officer in Yukon City?" I ask.

"Another woman, Lieutenant Em Davis, now the militia commander for Yukon."

"The forces that volunteer to stay behind will remain to guard the West Coast from further invasion," Chris says. "Meanwhile, I expect you to either find more forces in Alaska or seize weaponry that can help us in

25

this fight." He looks at me as he says this. "This is a *mission*. We need weapons or troops – or both. Whatever we can find. Are we clear, Commander Hart?"

"We're clear," I say.

He nods.

"Let's present the information to the troops, then," Andrew suggests. "Might as well get this out in the open."

I agree.

The secret is out.

***

In the end, the militia stays with Chris. I will be taking a detachment of thirty men into Alaska. We will look for reinforcements and check out the colony, making sure that Yukon City actually exists.

And Chris will remain in California, despite the odds stacked against him.

I know it. He knows it.

Yet he is resolute and stubborn in his determination to remain here, to keep fighting.

I look down at a map of Alaska on the meeting table. It is just Arlene and me. She sits in a chair, her fingers in a steeple, her brow knit.

"You're coming, right?" I ask.

"To Yukon City?" she replies. "No. I can't. Not yet."

"Why not? Manny is going. Aren't you going to –"

"Cassidy, there's more at stake here than just California. It's the survival of the rebellion on the West Coast. I have been in this fight since the beginning. I will see it through to the end – whatever that end may be."

"But what about Manny?" I ask. "And Elle?"

Arlene's expression doesn't flicker. It is stone.

"They will be okay without me."

I roll the map up.

"I don't like this division," I mutter.

"No one does. But it's necessary." Arlene sighs. "If we fall here in California, we will come to Yukon City. It will be a refuge for us. It will be a place to preserve what's left of us."

A cold shudder runs through my body.

"We won't go extinct," I say.

But that's a lie. So many things about our old civilization are already extinct.

There is no going back. Things will never be the same.

27

"I wish you would have told me about Yukon City sooner," I say. "Maybe we could have avoided the San Francisco fight."

"Maybe," Arlene whispers. "Maybe not."

A thought occurs to me, then.

"I want the specifics on the nuclear warheads that the Pacific Northwest Alliance had control of before Omega dropped the first bomb," I tell her. "And that's not a request, Arlene. That's an order."

She looks up at me, eyes weary and red.

"Yes," she says quietly. "Whatever you want, Commander."

I tuck the map in a pocket inside of my jacket and head toward the door. I need to pack my belongings and get ready to depart.

"This will change things," Arlene says absently, thrumming her fingers on the table. "You leaving – it will change everything. Especially for Chris."

I open the door.

"He's a soldier," I say, without turning back. "He'll survive."

Arlene doesn't respond.

I don't want her to.

Chapter Two

I sling my backpack and rifle over my shoulder, checking my appearance one last time in the mirror. Good to go. I leave my quarters and enter the wide, concrete hallways. Sector 27 is bursting with voices and energy. There are thirty of us heading to Alaska, the Angels of Death, worn but ready. I am one of them, and that knowledge thrills me as much as it frightens me.

I am saying goodbye to the only home I have ever known.

Farewell, California. We will meet again.

I hope.

I descend the stairwell and hit the main hall. Humvees and pickup trucks are rumbling. Some troops are already being taken to the airstrip. I stop dead in my tracks, staring at Uriah True. He is dressed in black, like me, his dark hair and eyes a shadow in the grayness of the bunker. His own backpack and rifle are slung across his broad shoulders.

"You're coming, then," I state.

"Yeah," he replies. "I follow my commander wherever she goes."

Behind him, I see Elle with Bravo, and beside them, Cheng. The Asian boy is taller than her, and he has cut his overgrown, shaggy hair. He is talking in hushed tones with Elle, who occasionally nods and smiles.

"Chris isn't coming," Uriah asks. It is a statement of fact, not a question.

"It's fine," I reply. "We'll be okay. We can do this."

"I know it will," he says. "I just want to make sure *you* know it."

"We've all aged a hundred years," I say suddenly. "Innocence is a thing of the past." I shrug. "Sorry, I'm rambling."

"It's okay." Uriah offers a slight smile. "You know I understand."

Yes, I know.

"See you onboard," I tell him.

"You bet."

I keep walking, passing Elle, Bravo and Cheng. Vera and Andrew are standing near a pickup, their gear in place. Vera looks better than she did when we first arrived. She looks rested, peaceful.

"Hey," Vera says.

I meet her blue eyes.

"We're going to make it," she goes on, her lips curving upward. "This change is a good thing."

I stop several feet in front of her.

"Yeah," I say. "Maybe."

"You know, you're a really good actress, because back in the meeting room you sounded like a fearless leader," she snorts. "Seriously, Cassidy. Snap out of it. We're all going to go to Yukon City, we'll find weapons or whatever they're hiding up there, and then we'll come back for Chris. It's cut and dried, simple. It's not like it's the end of the –"

"The end of the world?" I interrupt. "That's ironic."

She rolls her eyes.

"Giving you a pep talk is impossible."

I step forward and pull Vera into a tight hug. She stiffens, then slowly raises her hand to my back, offering several comforting pats. I close my eyes.

"We're a team," I whisper.

I step away. She blinks – hard.

"Okay, okay," she grumbles. "I get it."

But Andrew is smiling.

Elle, Bravo and Cheng approach the truck.

"Is this our sweet ride?" Elle asks.

"Yeah," Andrew replies. "And for the love of God, please don't make your dog sit on my lap this time. He smells."

"I'm crying crocodile tears, Lieutenant."

Elle swings her gear into the pickup bed, climbing into the backseat. Bravo follows her inside. Cheng assesses us.

"I just want to say, Commander Hart," he tells me, "that I think you are making the right decision."

"Thanks," I deadpan.

"You act as if my charming affirmations mean nothing to you. I'm wounded." He places a hand over his heart, chuckling.

"Shut up, idiot," Elle growls from the truck. "Get in."

A lazy grin spreads across Cheng's face. He gives me a sharp salute and climbs into the back seat. I shake my head. Cheng is a mystery – arrogant, charming and dangerous all at once. He might be the son of Veronica Klaus, but so far he has proven himself trustworthy. I still have my doubts, though.

Vera and Andrew get in the car. Uriah slides into the last spot.

"Where am I supposed to sit?" I say, raising an eyebrow.

Andrew gestures behind me and closes the door.

I turn around. Chris is standing there, tall and silent.

Andrew hits the accelerator and the pickup surges forward, into the long lineup of vehicles leaving the base.

I face Chris.

"I'll drive you," he says, simply.

Of course.

I follow him to a black Humvee idling at the corner of the base. I climb into the front passenger seat, throwing my gear into the backseat. Chris slides behind the wheel and spins the vehicle around, joining the end of the lineup.

I stare straight ahead, quiet.

Chris is wearing only a black shirt with his dark combat fatigues. The curves of his muscles press through the material. I absently touch the gold chain hanging around my neck, a gift from so long ago. An eternity, it seems.

"Well," I say. "You're driving me."

33

"Yeah." Chris clears his throat. His words are tight. We pull off the base, following the convoy through the open desert, racing at high speeds. The clouds are dark and ominous. "Here's the thing, Cassidy. Yukon City is a good idea. It really is. And I'm glad you're going. Arlene says they've got resources that we can tap into, and we need to explore that possibility."

I turn my head sharply.

"You're...glad?"

"Things are bad here in California," he continues. "Yukon City will need guidance and leadership from people who have been out in the war – who've seen what Omega does."

"And you don't think the survivor colony knows anything about that?"

"No. They've been there since the beginning, sheltered. They'll need your help."

I consider this.

"What if California completely falls, Chris?" I ask. "What then?"

"Then I'll join you in Alaska."

"And if not?"

"Then I expect you to bring something to kick Omega's butt in two months."

His words are matter-of-fact. Informational.

"I'll miss you," I say, looking out the window, tears filling my eyes.

Silence.

I feel Chris's fingers touch mine. I grasp his hand, firmly. He looks at me. His sharp green eyes are glazed. "I'll miss you, too," he says.

"We've always been together. All this time," I reply.

"Except when I was a prisoner of war."

"And I rescued you."

"Don't forget that I rescued you first from the labor camp."

"How could I?" I laugh. "You're my hero."

A sad, broken smile spreads across his face.

"I like to think so," he whispers.

We drive, the rolling black clouds boiling above our heads, the thundering engines of the convoy rattling in our ears, and the fear of separation settling in our stomachs like a lead weight.

"I'm sorry about what happened," he goes on, quietly. "Our fight, I mean. I didn't want to yell at you like that. I just...I just don't want to see you leave. But I understand why we have to do this. This is an important mission."

I squeeze his fingers.

"It will be okay," I say.

I feel like I've said that so much lately.

"Arlene is staying here," I continue. "Did you know that?"

"I did."

"Her loyalty to the militias and their secrets have torn her and Manny apart."

Chris casts a sideways glance at me.

"I know the feeling," he says.

I say nothing.

We finally come to a halt at an airfield several miles away from Sector 27. It is long and open, trails of tarmacs leading in every direction. A cargo plane is being loaded with the detachment of men who are accompanying me to Alaska.

"Two months for both of us," I say, turning to Chris. "Promise me. Not a day longer."

He raises an eyebrow.

"It's a promise." He looks at me, raising his hand to my cheek, brushing the skin softly with his calloused fingers. "But I expect you to come *back* here with reinforcements for me."

I smile faintly.

"I know," I say. "I'm going to try my best."

"I'm sending my mother and Isabel with you," Chris tells me, his hand fisted on the steering wheel. "I want them to be safe." He pauses. "You have to take care of them for me."

"Of course."

"They're all I have left. All three of you. You're it."

"And you're all *I* have." I tuck my loose hair behind my ear. "I love you."

I lean forward and kiss him, my nose pressed against the warmth of his skin, my lips tasting the coffee on his breath. He slides his hand behind my head and pulls me closer. I press my hands against his shoulders, grasping him tightly, as if I'm hanging on for dear life.

And perhaps I am.

"It's not goodbye, anyway," Chris says, gently, against my cheek. "It's just...*see you later.*"

I nod, fighting the heaving sob threatening to spill out of my chest.

"See you later," I echo.

He kisses me again. One last time. I pull away, looking into his eyes, nose to nose, a tear slipping down my face. He brushes it away with his finger.

I straighten my shoulders, resolute.

If I delay any further, I won't go. I'll lose my will.

I grab my gear, pull my scarf over my face, and open the Humvee door. The air is frigid and powerful. I walk around the front of the Humvee. Chris exits the vehicle and stands there, one boot on the running board, the intensity of his gaze searing.

"See you later," I whisper again.

He nods.

I turn away. I walk toward the planes.

I do not look back.

***

The plane that will take my comrades and me to Alaska is different than the rumbling, powerful cargo plane hauling the troops over state lines. Ours is a private plane, one that might have belonged to Arlene and Sky City once upon a time. A small, comfortable bird with plenty of room for my fellow militia leaders and guards.

I climb the steps, the wind whipping stray strands of hair into circles, and duck inside. It's warm and still. I set my gear down, waiting for the rest of the team to arrive.

"Sure you don't want to fly in the cockpit with me?" Manny asks.

His voice is quiet – halfhearted. He sits in the middle row of seats, his legs splayed apart, his hair hidden beneath a red bandana and a flight cap. His worn leather jacket is buttoned up, and a black scarf hangs around his neck.

"You know I'm not a big fan of flying," I say.

"Hmm. As I recall, I cured you of your fear of heights."

I cross my arms.

"Are you okay?" I ask.

Manny cracks a wry grin.

"Of course. I'm always okay." He folds his hands together. "It has merely dawned on me, my girl, that this separation...what we're doing here today...it will change everything. It means we're finally getting out of this hellhole. It means we might actually have some safety."

I lean against one of the leather seats.

"Manny," I say. "Convince Arlene to come with us. She's your wife. You love her. You don't have to leave without her. It's not a necessary sacrifice."

He looks up at me, his smile gone, his eyes bloodshot and weary.

"Isn't it, though?" he replies, standing up. I see him slip a metal flask back into his pocket, and I smell the faint stench of alcohol on his breath. "She's lied to me since the beginning. Since *before* the beginning, actually." He releases a harsh laugh. "Her loyalty to Sky City and the militias has always taken priority over me. Always."

I tilt my head, wondering how someone like Arlene and someone like Manny ended up together in the first place: a cool and cunning woman and a wild-eyed, passionate pilot with a taste for whiskey.

"If you love her," I tell him, "you should stay here with her."

Manny takes a step forward, then sinks back into the seat again.

"No," he sighs. "Not this time. I've always functioned very well on my own. We're independent creatures, Arlene and me. Like two old horses in a pasture. We stick to our own grass and when we cross paths, we nuzzle a little and then go our separate ways again." He winks at me. "Going to Yukon City doesn't mean I don't love the woman, my girl. It just means we're going our separate ways this time. Maybe for the last time. I don't know."

He looks sad. I don't know how he can stand it.

Or maybe I do.

Chris's still, solemn face flashes through my head.

We do what we must to protect the people we love.

"I understand," I say. "Leaving Chris is hard for me, too."

"Ah, you'll be back together again in no time," Manny grins. "You always are."

I sit down.

"Yeah," I say. "You're right about that."

"Arlene and I have been different from the start," he goes on, absent, rambling. "When we were young, there was nothing that could stop her from getting what she wanted. Nothing." He laughs. "And I was just a pilot. All I wanted to do was fly. Fly to the moon and back and take her with me." He shakes his head. "It was a good dream, Cassidy. A good dream." He leans forward, bowing his head. "And the dream is over, now. It died when the world died."

A long, impossible silence stretches between us.

"Ready to go?" Elle announces, stepping inside the plane, Bravo at her side.

Manny snaps up, all traces of sorrow and broken dreams erased from his face. His dark, wrinkled face turns into a smile.

"Ready, willing and able!" Manny exclaims.

Elle's pale cheeks are rosy and pinched. Cheng follows closely behind her, a dark shadow. "I don't like flying," Cheng mutters.

"Hmm," Manny replies. "That's so sad."

"I sense unbridled sarcasm, old man," Cheng says, rolling his eyes.

"First of all, I am not *old*," Manny replies. "I am *aged*, like a fine wine. I've said that before and I mean it. And second, by the time we're done, you'll love flying as much as I do." He jerks his thumb at me. "Ask her. I cured her of *her* fear."

"Not entirely." I grin, remembering how we crashed a helicopter in Los Angeles. How we fell from the sky, burning, and nearly died. How I survived a

HALO jump from twenty thousand feet into the frigid mountains.

So, yeah. Flying is not on my list of top ten things to do for leisure.

Mrs. Young steps into the cabin, her graying hair pulled into a loose ponytail. She is bundled in a big jacket and boots. Isabel is clutching her arm, eyes bright with curiosity.

"Hey," I say.

I haven't spoken to either of them since our arrival at Sector 27.

"Cassidy," Mrs. Young – Margaret – replies. "We're coming with you."

She steps forward and folds me into a hug.

"It's not permanent," she whispers into my ear. "Chris loves you too much."

I smile, sad.

"I know he does," I answer. "Don't worry, this is a good move for us."

Vera and Andrew enter the cabin, their boots thumping on the stairs.

"I think I'm going to be really annoyed with you," Vera hisses, stalking toward the back of the plane, brushing past us, plopping down on a seat, looking angrily at Andrew. "Don't sit next to me."

Andrew swallows, pale.

"I suggested that we should maybe stay behind instead of going to Yukon City," he tells me in a low voice.

"*Not* happening!" Vera snaps.

I shake my head.

"Well, you two lovebirds need to work it out, because I'm not going to listen to you fight the whole flight north," I say, firmly. "Don't make this my problem."

"Nobody asked *you*, Doctor Phil," Vera huffs.

I shake my head. Elle and Cheng have settled into seats toward the front. I bend down and stroke the fur on Bravo's head. His deep, wise eyes smile at mine.

"How's your dog?" I ask Elle. "Does he ever get tired of this?"

"Of the war?" Elle shrugs. "No. He's a military working dog. This is what he does."

I am still kneeling next to Bravo when Uriah enters the plane.

"Bonding with the dog?" Uriah asks.

"Yeah," I say. "He likes me."

44

"He likes everyone."

"Not *everyone*," Elle mutters.

Uriah takes a seat apart from everyone else. Andrew and Vera are talking in tense, hushed tones in the back of the cabin. Manny looks out the window. I see Arlene standing at the edge of the tarmac, staring at the plane. Chris is nearby, doing the same thing.

I look away and sit down. The door closes and seals, eliminating the outside noise.

"We'll be back," Elle tells me, smiling tightly. "This isn't the end. Not yet."

"Not yet," I reply.

Manny sidles into the cockpit and checks things one final time. According to our plan, we will arrive at the Way Station in Alaska in six or seven hours. Only Manny knows the location. In fact, the pilots are the only ones who know where the coordinates for the first Way Station is.

It makes it harder for Omega traitors who may have infiltrated our ranks to turn this information in to their superiors. But I'm hoping that our traitors are long gone. What remains of the California militias is small but powerful – bound together by blood and tragedy and loss.

Our numbers have changed, but our resolve has only gotten stronger.

"What if we get to Yukon City and nobody is there?" Elle asks me, biting her lip. "I mean, what if they're gone or destroyed? We have no way of knowing until we get there, right?"

"I guess not."

"Then we will have gone all that way for nothing."

"That's not true. We have to try."

She considers this.

"So if there *are* people there, and they *do* want to volunteer to help fight Omega," she says, "then we bring them back with us to California? Just like that?"

"Yes."

"And if they don't want to come?"

"Then we look somewhere else."

"But what about weapons? Arlene keeps saying that they've got weapons we can use. What kind of weapons do you think she's talking about?"

"I don't know," I say. But it's a lie. I have an inkling.

It strikes me in this moment that if we fail in our mission, we may be forced to go elsewhere to look for recruits.

"Would we go to the East Coast?" Elle asks. "Or would we leave the country altogether?"

"I don't know," I say, honestly. "None of us know what the rest of the world looks like right now. Maybe it's just North America that's at war. Maybe we can find more allies that can help us."

The words leave my mouth, but I'm not entirely sure that I believe them.

I have a gut feeling that the rest of the world is just as embroiled in this apocalypse as we are. It only makes our situation more desperate...more terrifying.

"I don't care where we go," Vera comments from behind me. "I just want to get out of this godforsaken state. I'm so sick of California. The same fight, over and over again. The death and the destruction. I want to put it behind me."

I sit down, my eyes drawn to the window once again.

Neither Arlene nor Chris have moved.

"California is a terrible thing to lose," Elle whispers. She leans her head against Cheng's shoulder.

He props his boot up on the chair in front of him, pensive.

"I'm never coming back here," Vera says. "Never."

I hear the acidity in her voice, and I understand her bitterness, her sorrow. This state holds more sadness for me than happiness, now. At first, when we were fighting against Omega, it was a battle for our homes – for our families. Now, our families are gone and our memories are tarnished with visions of slaughtered men, women and children. We've lost our connection to what makes us normal and civilized. The climate of war and rebellion is a constant.

"What if the militias need you to fight here again?" I ask her, quietly. "If we find reinforcements, I'll need you to come back here with me and help lead them."

"Then that's too bad. I've paid my dues. I've fought."

"The war isn't over yet, Vera. Not by a long shot."

"Believe me, I know."

I turn around and face her. Her arms are folded over her chest; her eyes are flashing.

"You wouldn't leave me to fight alone," I say. "I know you wouldn't."

Vera shakes her head and stares out the window. She doesn't answer.

"Oh, I almost forgot!" Elle exclaims suddenly. "Arlene wanted me to give this to you."

She unzips her backpack and pulls a blank manila envelope out. She hands it to me. I set it in my lap, puzzled. "What is this?" I ask.

"Don't know. She just said to give it to you." Elle shrugs.

I flip it over, tracing my finger along the curve of the seal.

Outside, Arlene has turned her back on the tarmac, finally retreating to the convoy. Chris remains still, never taking his eyes off our plane.

I open the envelope. There are three sheets of paper. The first one reads:

Destroy After Reading

I frown, looking at the next page:

Cassidy,

Here is the information on the nuclear weapons. Other than myself, only five militia leaders know about this. Chris is one of those five, as I'm sure you have discovered already. My request to you is simple: use this knowledge wisely. If it falls into the

wrong hands, it could destroy everything – the whole world, actually. Don't take that lightly.

Many nuclear weapons have gone missing or were seized by Omega during the first wave of the invasion, shortly after the EMP. However, shortly before the Collapse, several of our own who, for the purpose of protecting their identities, shall not be named, relocated the nuclear warheads on the West Coast for safekeeping, to protect them from falling into the enemy's hands.

The remaining warheads are our last line of defense against a total Omega takeover. And I do mean last, *Cassidy. They have bombed us, but returning fire could result in total nuclear annihilation.*

Memorize the locations listed, and destroy this information when you are done.

I pray that Yukon City is everything we hope it is. Our survival depends on it.

- *Arlene*

I slip the last page on top.

CLASSIFIED

Location of remaining nuclear warheads is as follows:

Mexico City, Mexico (PNWA Stronghold)
Area 51, Nevada
Phoenix, Arizona
Seattle (Destroyed, Omega nuclear attack)
Alaska (Location Unknown)

The list goes on, naming cities and towns across the United States and the entire North American continent. Many of them are labeled as "missing" or "destroyed."

How do you destroy a nuclear warhead? I think, raising an eyebrow.

You don't, not really. You can disarm it, but other than that...

My mind works quickly. Having a huge nuclear arsenal at our disposal could change the tide of the war. Maybe if Omega knew that we were capable of returning fiery destruction straight to their front door, we'd have a chance at survival.

Or maybe...it would do exactly what Arlene said: Nuclear annihilation.

Besides, where would we even send the warheads? We don't even know where Omega is based.

"What'd she write to you?" Vera asks from behind me.

I slide the papers back into the envelope.

"It's personal," I say.

I seal it.

Manny yells, "Everybody buckle their seatbelts and hang on. We're about to fly away from the Golden State!"

He laughs manically.

I wonder how he does it – how he detaches himself from the tragedy of leaving Arlene and finds it within himself to grin and laugh.

The plane rumbles to life. I grip the envelope and look out the window. I can see Chris, arms folded across his broad chest, his eyes hidden behind black shooting glasses. What is he thinking right now? What am *I* thinking?

I love you. I love you so much. I'll see you. Soon.

The plane rolls forward, bouncing slightly with every roll on the tarmac. The plane turns, and Manny begins coasting. I hear him talking into the radio, occasionally throwing comments back into the cabin. I don't pay attention. I can't stop watching Chris.

I don't want to look away.

The plane picks up speed. The asphalt and the desert turn into a blur as the plane lifts off the ground. My throat drops into my stomach as we ascend, higher, higher, the desert floor becoming a distant speck.

Goodbye, California. I fought for you. I gave you everything I had.

I close my eyes and lean my head against the seat, praying under my breath that everybody will make it to the Way Station in one piece.

Chapter Three

Three hours into the flight, I look out the window. All I can see is a blanket of black, angry clouds. They cover the sky like a quilt, blocking the earth from view. Here, the sun is shining, pure and bright, casting brilliant golden light across the blackness.

"It's so beautiful!" Elle exclaims.

I stand up, Arlene's envelope tucked into the inside pocket of my jacket, and walk to the pilot's cockpit. Manny is sitting with his headset on.

"Ah, finally break down and come to beg me to teach you to fly?" he asks, grinning.

"Let me think," I say. "Oh wait. That would be a *no*."

"You've disappointed me, my girl."

"Sorry. I'm just a bundle of disappointments today." I sit in the empty co-pilot's seat. The control panel is complicated but, like everything else in life, I'm sure I could learn to fly with practice.

"Where are we right now?" I ask.

"Ah, that would be the *sky*," Manny quips.

"Ha. Ha."

He adjusts his headset. "We're right over Washington."

My heart sinks.

Washington was hit hard with a nuclear bomb. Beneath the clouds, I can only imagine the blackened devastation of the earth's crust. I am glad that we can't see all the way to the ground.

"How much longer until we get there?" I ask.

"Well, little girl, we'll get there *when we get there.*" He laughs at his own joke. "Around five hours. Maybe more. Maybe less. Depends on whether or not we encounter any trouble."

"Thanks," I say.

I stand up and wander back into the cabin. Margaret Young is sitting in the back, Isabel asleep on her shoulder. Elle is playing tic-tac-toe with Cheng, and Vera and Andrew are still arguing.

I sigh and plop down in the chair beside Uriah.

"Lonely?" he asks, ghosting a smile.

"Restless," I reply. I touch the collar of my jacket. I want to tell him about the information that Arlene gave me. I want to discuss the burden with him, the knowledge. But I cannot, because I can't break the trust. I can't tell the secret.

"We're taking a big risk here," I mutter.

"I wouldn't worry about it," he says. "Let's focus on getting to Yukon City, and finding some recruits."

"Right."

Uriah playfully nudges my shoulder.

"Don't look so depressed," he says.

"I'm not depressed. I'm thinking."

"Same difference."

"Shut up." But I smile. "I'm glad you chose to come with us."

"I know." He tilts his head. "You needed someone other than Vera to talk to."

I laugh.

"That's very true." I lean back in the seat. "I hate leaving California, but at the same time, I feel like a weight has been lifted off my shoulders already – not being there is freeing."

"You'll always be tethered to California," Uriah observes, "as long as Chris is there."

I frown.

"But you're doing the right thing," he goes on.

"I'd like to think so."

The cabin shakes and shudders. I inhale and grip the seats.

"Ladies and gentlemen," Manny announces over the intercom, "please fasten your seatbelts. We are experiencing a little turbulence. Let's hope we don't all crash and die."

He cackles.

Click.

"You know," I tell Uriah, "my dad used to be terrified of flying. He was kind of claustrophobic. Didn't like being locked in." I smile wistfully, thinking of my father. "I miss him."

"He was a good man." Uriah shifts in his seat. "He was a great commander."

"He was." I look at him. "Do you ever wonder what you would be doing if the Collapse hadn't happened?"

"No." He shakes his head. "That kind of thing is deadly. You start getting nostalgic. Nostalgia doesn't do me any good. It just makes me weak."

"It does not. It makes you remember what we're fighting for."

"It reminds me that everything I was – everything I knew – is gone."

I drop my gaze to my feet.

"I guess."

I stand up and go into the small restroom in the back of the plane. I stand in front of the mirror and stare at my face – so much sharper and older than it used to be. I pull the envelope out of my jacket and slide the papers out. I read the cities to myself, over and over again, until I have memorized it.

I set the papers in the sink and pop a packet of matches out of my pocket. I strike a match. The tiny flame glows brightly in the dim light. I hold the fire to the edges of the paper. The flames seize the documents and consume the pages, disintegrating every scrap.

I watch the fire eat the words until there is nothing left but a pile of ashes. I flip the sink on, and a stream of cool water washes the mess away.

I put the matches back in my pocket.

Done.

Chapter Four

Alaska.

It's almost four o'clock in the afternoon, but the ground below is cloaked in a wispy twilight.

"Why is it so dark?" Isabel asks, alarmed.

"In Alaska, they have long periods of time where it's completely sunny or totally dark," Andrew answers, leaning into the aisle. "It's the winter solstice. They'll have about sixty or so days of darkness before the sun starts to make a reappearance."

"But it's not totally dark," Vera points out. "It's like a twilight darkness. You can still see in it – it's just shadowy."

"Exactly," Andrew agrees.

Looking down on the world below us, I can make out the outline of the coast, different shades of black, blue and gray.

"People here *like* living in darkness?" Isabel remarks.

"There are worse things," Elle points out.

"I guess."

Manny has begun our descent. In the far off distance, I can see tiny, twinkling lights. Lights meant specifically for us, to help us land the aircraft in the correct spot. The lights are blue from this angle, branching in multiple directions, patterns that Manny can read.

"Prepare for landing," he says into the intercom.

I sit straight in my seat.

"I hope he can land this thing without killing us all," Cheng comments. "I would like to live until at *least* Christmas."

The plane rumbles a little, quaking with the force of the wind outside.

Manny is talking into the radio, throwing back comments to the passengers in the cabin. For the most part, I tune him out, watching the dark earth below us loom closer and closer. As we descend, I notice a slight tinge of orange and pink light over the horizon, past what appears to be a rocky mountain range.

"I thought you said it doesn't get sunny this time of year," I say.

"It's called civil twilight," Andrew replies. "It lasts for a short amount of time, lights everything up like a nightlight, then disappears."

Bump, bump, bump.

The wheels of the plane make contact with the runway. I feel that familiar sensation of weight in my chest, pressing me forward and backward all at once. I take a deep breath. We are coasting, now. We are on the ground again.

I close my eyes.

Step one, complete. We made it in one piece.

"Easy, easy!" Manny yells from the cockpit. "Everybody stay seated. I see a welcoming party on the tarmac."

I bolt out of my seat anyway. I step into the cockpit, peering out the windows. The runway lights are shedding just enough of a glow on the small tarmac to illuminate the small building sitting on the left. In front of the edifice, a group of people have gathered to watch our plane. Around us, the Chugach Mountains loom into the sky, capped with pure white snow, dark and ominous – silent and powerful accolades to the sheer might of the terrain of Alaska.

Eventually Manny takes the plane to a docking area on the side of the building. The engines slowly cut out. I walk into the cabin, grab my backpack, button my jacket, and keep my rifle close to my chest.

"You and me go first," I tell Uriah.

He nods, understanding.

"Margaret," I say, "stay here until we give the go-ahead."

Elle and Cheng rise. Bravo gets to his feet, sensing the anticipation for the moment when the plane door hisses open and we're greeted by the men outside.

God, I hope Arlene is right about this place, I think.

Manny stands silently in the doorway of the cockpit, nodding.

"It will be okay, my girl," he says. "These people can be trusted."

"I hope so," Elle whispers.

Cheng squeezes her hand. They share a secret glance. The door opens. I keep my finger hovering above the trigger of the rifle as it does, standing just to the side of the opening. My first instinct is to find cover. The steps roll down, and I feel a rush of cold, pure air blow into the cabin.

Alaska.

I take the first step outside, Uriah behind my shoulder.

Fifty feet away from the foot of the steps, militiamen are gathered, dressed in dark fatigues. There are ten. In front, a young woman with chocolate skin and cool, intelligent eyes stands with a working dog on a leash.

I descend the steps, stomach tight, mouth dry.

Uriah follows me, and then Elle, Cheng and Bravo. Vera, Andrew and Manny emerge next. I stand, motionless, mimicking the expression on the dark woman's face.

At last, she breaks the silence.

"Welcome to Alaska," she says. "Are you the commanding officer?"

"I am," I reply. "Commander Cassidy Hart."

"Nice to meet you, Commander." She bows her head. "I'm Commander Em Davis, and these are my men. We're here to act as a greeting party."

The group of men standing behind her is silent, but they issue a sharp salute when she introduces them.

"We come on the word of Arlene Costas," I go on.

She raises an eyebrow. Her dog looks up at her. "This is your team?"

"Yes," I reply. "Lieutenant Uriah True, Sergeant Elle Costas and her partner Cheng, Sergeant Bravo, Lieutenant Manny Costas, and Lieutenants Vera Wright and Andrew Decker."

Em's eyes widen.

"Sergeant Bravo?"

"You know my dog?" Elle asks.

Bravo huffs.

"He and India trained together, once," Em says, gesturing at her dog, a beautiful German Shepherd with a fair coat and dark speckles of color near her nose. "God, this apocalypse has made the world a lot smaller than it used to be." She shakes her head. "Who else is with you?"

"We have two civilians on this plane," I say. "And I've got a transport of thirty men coming this way."

"Good," she announces. She crosses the distance between us and offers her hand. I shake it. Her grip is firm. "President Bacardi sent me. My job is to get you to Yukon City safe and sound."

I say, "Thank you."

I tell Uriah to get Margaret and Isabel out of the plane. Manny stuffs his hands into his pockets, an agitated expression on his face.

"Take us inside," I command Em. "The rest of our troops will be arriving shortly."

She nods.

We follow Em through the wispy darkness. I feel strangely disoriented. The darkness is similar to the dusky light of the early morning – I can see everything around me, but it feels as if no time is passing, because of the lack of sunshine.

The building is a small, squat edifice with two double doors and large windows facing the airfield. We walk inside. It's warm, lit with orange lights that flicker slightly as the generator pulses. The interior of the building is little more than an empty room with benches.

"This is our *terminal,* if you will," Em explains, grinning slightly. "We periodically process incoming refugees and survivors from out of state here before taking them to Yukon. Usually, we put them through a lengthy interrogation to make sure we're not letting any Omega plants into our safe zone."

"Have you ever had any trouble?" Andrew asks. "With spies, I mean?"

"Let's just say we've never had an Omega spy get past this terminal, as far as we know," Em replies. "Yukon City is the most valuable asset the militias have left. We do everything we can to protect it."

I can only imagine the fate that awaits an Omega spy once they are found out here.

"What's the status of California?" Em asks, furrowing her brow.

"California's coastline has fallen to Omega," I reply. "I'm here on a mission."

"And what mission is that?"

"I'm sorry, but that's classified information." I ghost a smile.

Em tilts her head.

"We have the space and supplies to support your men," she says, "but President Bacardi will want to speak with you once we arrived at the colony."

"I'll be happy to talk with her."

"Last time I was in California, everything was hitting the fan," Em replies. "It was bad. I came up here to escape – it was the best thing I ever did. I can help more people up here than I could down there."

"That's the conclusion I came to," I say.

"We have vehicles for you and your men," she continues. "We'll move you to Yukon City through the tunnel – we call it Maynard Tunnel, because it runs through the Maynard Mountain."

"Sounds good," I say.

"You can wait here until the rest of your men arrive," Em tells us. "I need to have a word with the Sky Watchmen."

She takes her dog and leaves the building. I turn to Uriah.

"Well?" I say.

"She seems trustworthy," he replies.

"My thoughts exactly."

"Why would anybody want to live where it's *dark all the time*?" Vera mutters, frowning. "It's just not natural."

"Vera," I say. "Shut up."

"You know what, Hart –"

"No. Just stop. I don't want to listen to you complain the whole way to Yukon." A slight smile touches my lips. "I shouldn't have to remind you that you're not twelve years old."

Vera's cheeks fill with color and she stalks away, to the window.

I remind myself that Vera has been through a lot of trauma in the last week, too, and it is only natural to complain a little bit. On the other hand, she is a lieutenant, and as such, it's her job to perform in a mature manner – especially in front of young soldiers like Elle and civilian refugees like Isabel and Margaret Young.

She will adjust.

I don't like the darkness, either, but it's better than being in California.

Chris is in California.

I shake myself.

Two months. Two months. Two months.

Isabel sits quietly next to Margaret on one of the benches. I watch her closely. I remember the days when Isabel was full of uncontained energy – when her bright sense of humor and vitality would light up a room.

Ever since her adoptive father was killed and Omega dropped their first nuclear bomb on the West Coast, she has been quiet – morose. She clings to

Margaret like someone clings to a life preserver. Not only that, she seems to have drifted away from me, too. In her eyes, I am someone to be feared.

Somehow, I have become something I never knew I could.

I have become a symbol of fear. A symbol of rebellion.

"What if they don't want us there?" Elle whispers, leaning close to me. "What if Yukon City sees us as a threat?"

"They won't," I tell her with confidence I don't feel.

"I hope you're right."

"I am."

I walk to the windows and look across the airfield, the twinkling, bluish lights pointed toward the sky. I wonder if they are always lit, or if the Sky Watchmen only turn them on when they are expecting visitors.

"If we get to Yukon," Uriah whispers, "and they turn us away, we should stay anyway. We'll make it work. What are they going to do if we refuse to go, anyway? Kill us?"

I give him a sharp look.

"They're going to accept us," I say. "We're all on the same side, you know."

"I'm just saying. It's a possibility. We should be prepared for it."

"I know." I trace my finger on the cold window pane, drawing a circle. "This place has supposedly been made for people like us – if they turned us away...well, that would be almost immoral. They have a duty to perform, and so do we."

The words roll off my tongue, but I don't have a lot of faith in them.

Yukon City could be everything we dreamed of – or everything we fear.

We find ourselves sitting on the benches, tired and jet-lagged from the long flight, nervous about what waits for us at Yukon City, and missing what we have left behind.

***

My detachment of men arrives in the cargo plane. I step outside with Uriah as Em Davis and her men evaluate each and every one of the troops. They are lined out the door with their duffel bags and gear, tired and weary.

Inside, every soldier is briefly interrogated. So far, nobody has been booted.

Not one. Not yet.

"We're going to be here all night," Uriah mutters.

"Actually, it's only a little after lunchtime," I remind him. "It's just dark here."

"Well, speaking of lunch," he goes on. "Let's go grab some."

"I don't think so, Uriah. Not right now."

"We got nothing better to do." A devilish smile appears on his otherwise dark face. "Come on."

I tap the holster on my belt.

I *am* hungry.

I turn and follow him back toward the plane Manny flew to get us here. We climb the steps and slip inside the cabin. Uriah drops his backpack on the seat and pulls out his supplies – beef jerky, vacuum-sealed cheese and water bottles. I sit down on the floor, my boots propped up on the armrests of the seats, and pull my own food out. I unwrap the homemade beef jerky and tear it with my teeth, feeling the rubbery, salty grit of the meat on my tongue.

"Remember when you could just walk out the front door and go grab a sandwich for lunch?" I say, wistful. "Or a large order of french fries? Those were the days."

"I never ate fast food," Uriah answers.

"What? Are you serious? What's wrong with you?"

"Nothing," Uriah replies, half-laughing. "I just thought it was gross."

"Gross, maybe. But delicious? Absolutely."

"I have to remind myself that you grew up in the *city*. Country people like me just made our own dinner at home. Butter from our own cows, eggs from our own chickens –"

"And clothes from the wool of your own sheep," I grin. "Whatever."

Uriah shrugs.

"You know that whatever happens here," Uriah says, "I'm with you. All the way."

"I know." I touch his hand. "Thank you."

He squeezes my fingers between his – fingers long and slender, twice the length of mine. I look at our hands, reminding myself that before all of this madness

– before the end of the world – Uriah was a young man in a small town, a hotshot rookie cop.

How would his life be different if the Collapse had never happened?

"Do you ever think about what you would be doing if this hadn't happened?" I ask, quietly. "I mean, if the Collapse had never happened and everything was normal again?"

"I told you, I don't think about what was or could have been."

"Do you think you would be married? Or maybe living in a big city?"

Uriah shakes his head.

"I really don't care," he says. "It doesn't matter anymore."

"I would have gone into forensic science," I go on. "Something along those lines. Maybe law enforcement, maybe something else. I don't know."

"It wouldn't have surprised me at all," Uriah comments. "Sometimes I think you were made for this life. Like this apocalypse brought the best out of you when it brought the worst out of everyone else."

I say nothing. This apocalypse has not brought the best out of me – not always. I have killed many

73

people, and I cannot wash the thought of bloody vengeance against Omega out of my head. The idea plays like an audio loop, constantly repeating itself, bouncing against the insides of my skull.

"I'm not who I used to be," I say. "Sometimes, I wonder where that girl went. If she's even still inside me."

"She's there," Uriah replies, leaning closer. "She's just older and wiser, now."

I look at him, holding his gaze, his dark eyes glinting in the dim lighting.

"I hope so," I say.

Elle walks inside the cabin.

"I figured you'd be in here," she says. "I think we're ready to go."

I stand up.

"Let's get this party started," I mutter.

Chapter Five

Em Davis is standing near the door to the lead Humvee in the lineup of convoys. Uriah and I approach her and her dog, India. She flashes a curious expression.

"I hope you're not claustrophobic," she says.

"You're worried the tunnel is going to freak me out?" I ask.

"Yeah, kind of."

"That's cute." I grin. "We'll all be fine."

Em shrugs and gets into the lead vehicle. Uriah and I follow. Isabel and Margaret ride in the vehicle behind us, along with Andrew and Vera. Manny, Elle, Cheng and Bravo are in the SUV behind them. I climb into the backseat of the lead Humvee. Uriah and I keep our rifles upright between our knees, peering through the windows.

In front of us, there is a triangular rooftop cupping the entrance to the tunnel. It looks tiny and discreet. Railroad tracks plunge into the darkness.

"Hey, I thought this tunnel was for automobiles," Uriah says.

Em twists in her seat, smiling.

"Yeah, before the Collapse, they shared the tunnel with cars and trains," she replies. "These days, we just use it as a way to get in and out of the city without being seen."

The driver of our vehicle is tall and stoic, never smiling, never saying a word. The Humvee rolls forward and Em says something into the radio. I wiggle my fingers, not realizing that I have been clenching my fists.

Relax, I think. *We're with the militia and nobody knows we're here. We're safe.*

We keep moving forward, until we plunge into the darkness of the mountain tunnel. The walls loom all around us, small and tight. It's pitch-black, darker than the darkest night. The headlights from the Humvee carve a sharp beam into the tunnel as we move forward, briskly whisking ahead at a steady speed of thirty miles per hour.

"My men will seal the tunnel from their side once we're through," Em explains, turning to me, stroking the fur on India's head. "We like to keep the entrance as hidden as possible."

"Do you have men guarding the tunnel entrance around the clock?" I ask.

"Absolutely. No security measure is too much – we don't take any risks here."

"Good," I say.

Maybe these people actually have their act together.

As we drive through the tunnel, the walls seem to close in around us. I can't help but wonder what would happen if we were to get stuck in here – would we be sealed inside, trapped inside a giant, two-mile-long coffin?

I shudder and push the thought away.

It seems to take forever, but eventually, we pop out of the tunnel. The dreamlike darkness of Alaska suddenly seems bright and welcoming. I exhale, and as I do so, I see Em Davis's lips twist into a slight smirk in the rearview mirror.

Whatever.

Whittier stands before us. As we pull out of the tunnel, the first thing that strikes me is the beauty. Whittier is a small strip of land situated in a sheltered harbor, with mountains looming on all sides of it. It is nestled in the back of the bay, looking out over deep blue water. A few old, black submarines bob in the water, dormant and silent. I see a couple of buildings here and there, but mostly, there are just trees and hills, and then towering mountains and piles of white snow.

"It looks like a fairytale," I whisper. "It's beautiful."

"We're proud of it," Em states. "Before the Collapse, cruise ships used to come and dock at Whittier. It was popular with photographers, hikers, honeymooners. You know, a big tourist draw. But it's so hard to find, as you can see."

The little city is dark, impossible to spot from the sky, keeping them safe from possible Omega surveillance. The convoy takes a sharp right and roars down a long, curving road that parallels the harbor.

I see boats bobbing in the water, along with small, icy glaciers and sheets of sparkling ice. It is an ethereal, alien landscape, full of wonder and surprises. It looks like nothing I have ever seen before in California.

"Welcome to Yukon City," Em says.

Up ahead, I see a checkpoint, heavily guarded by Alaskan National Guardsmen. There is a tall chain-link fence topped with coils of sharp barbed wire. Beyond the fence is a maze of railroad tracks, and just further on are two large buildings spaced apart. They are the biggest buildings in sight, and they dominate the small skyline.

The convoy rolls to a halt. They check in with Em Davis.

After they confirm with the guardhouse, they lift the gate and our convoy keeps moving through.

"Small town," I comment.

"Small but tight," Em replies. "That building on the left, the one that looks like a compound?" She points to a sprawling edifice, standing tall against the backdrop of trees and snow. "That's the Hodge Building – we call them the Begich Towers now. And the building over there on the right? That's the Buckner Building. We house civilian refugees in Buckner, and the Begich Towers are where we're housing militiamen."

We rumble through a small tunnel that pops out next to a city park and a campground packed with thick canvas tents and RVs. I see civilians everywhere – men, women and children.

I smell the heavy, woodsy scent of burning campfires and hear the laughter of children. I look at Uriah. He raises an eyebrow, but says nothing. We make a sharp turn and head straight for the Begich Towers.

"These civilians in the campground," I say. "Where are they from?"

"Everywhere. Most of them are from the big cities like Anchorage – survivors of the initial collapse. They saw the world going down in flames so they came here. The militias did a lot to help relocate wandering survivors to this place." She shrugs. "We obviously don't have enough room to house everybody in the Buckner Building," Em replies. "In fact, there just aren't a lot of buildings in Yukon City *period.* So most of the people here live in their RVs, their trailers, their motor homes...whatever they have. It's better than being alone, or in Omega's crosshairs."

"I was told that Yukon City has an established government," I say.

"Well, yeah. I already mentioned President Bacardi."

"And the senate?"

"Some of them were former public officials. Others were just...well, they were leaders within the civilian refugee camps and they were elected because the people trusted them."

"And the militias – the National Guard?"

"The militias are under my control. The National Guard has their own commander – Colonel Wilcox." She sniffs. "He's gruff, but he gets the job done." She tilts her head. "And then there are the Roamers. They have their own little fortress, on the outskirts of the city. They keep to themselves, but they're dangerous fighters. We're lucky to have them as an ally."

"Roamers?" I echo.

"Yeah. A group of religious zealots," Em answers. "They came in several months ago, a good quarter of their men wounded or dying. They'd been in a fight with Omega. They came here to seek religious asylum, so to speak. So they live here, now. Isolated, but ready."

I bite my lip. There are a lot of different players here in Yukon City.

"One more question," I say.

"Yeah?"

"The name. Yukon City. You guys are nowhere near the Yukon."

"It was Mauve's idea," Em shrugs. "The idea is that Yukon City isn't just in Whittier or Alaska. It's not just another refuge. We're supposed to be the ultimate refuge – it's supposed to convey hope. Yukon City sounds hopeful, don't you think?"

I don't reply. I don't know.

The convoy comes to a stop at last right in front of the Begich Towers. We exit the Humvee and step into the icy air blowing in from the harbor. It is bone-cold, the ancient frigidity of the arctic. I grip the strap on my rifle, watching Vera, Andrew, Elle, Cheng, Bravo and Manny climb out of their vehicles, along with the rest of my detachment.

It's a simple building – fourteen levels of windows.

"Condominiums," Em explains.

Thick clouds are hanging over the tips of the mountains, miring Whittier and Yukon City in a blanket of shadows. I feel like I've taken a step into another world.

Other vehicles are parked all around the towers. Dead weeds stand in icy clumps. And, standing near the corner with a small force of men dressed in forest green fatigues, is a woman. She is extremely tall – at least six feet. Dark brown hair is braided down her back. Her features are pointed and sharp – she wears loose jeans, boots and a thick jacket.

"That's President Mauve Bacardi," Em says, quietly. "She's anxious to meet you."

"Anxious?" I echo.

"We don't get a lot of outsiders from the militias. We get survivors, but not para-military units. Not transferring here, anyway." Em stops herself, like she's afraid she has said too much. "Come on, I'll introduce you."

I follow her across the cracked asphalt. Up close I see that Mauve is maybe fifty years old, at the most. Deep wrinkles carve out the spaces around her eyes.

"President Bacardi," Em says. "Mission accomplished."

Mauve raises an eyebrow.

"Commander Hart?" she says. Her voice is deep and raspy.

"Yes." I offer my hand. "It's nice to meet you, President."

She looks at my hand. She doesn't take it.

"You've come a long way to get here," she says instead. "You must be tired."

"We're fine," I reply.

"Your men will be properly accommodated in these towers." She gestures to the building. "But I would like to have a word with you, Commander Hart."

I sense something in Mauve's voice – anger? Fear?

"Very well," I agree.

I nod at Uriah. He walks over.

"President Bacardi," I say. "Lieutenant Uriah True."

She says nothing.

"I'm going to speak with the president inside," I tell Uriah. "Take over for me until I come back."

"Yes, Commander," Uriah says, but he throws a discerning glance at Mauve.

I leave my men behind, gathering their duffel bags, backpacks and weapons from the vehicles. Em Davis flanks me as I follow Mauve into the building, surrounded on all sides by the forest-green troops. We step into a long, narrow hallway, lit by generator-powered lights. We keep moving, stopping at a huge room at the end. Mauve and her guards sweep inside – Mauve is so tall that she nearly has to duck to keep from hitting her head on the doorway.

Inside, there is a large room with two couches, a desk in the corner, and a small window overlooking the snowy parking lot. Nothing flashy. A small pellet stove burns in the corner, emitting warmth.

"Leave us," Mauve commands, sitting behind the desk.

Behind her, there is a row of bookshelves covered in dust. The guards silently file out of the room. Commander Davis remains rooted to the spot with India.

"Have a seat," Mauve offers, a slight smile touching her lips.

I slowly lower myself onto the couch, resting my fist on the armrest. Em remains standing near the window, her lips pressed into a thin line.

"Tell me, Commander Hart," Mauve says. "We don't receive any communications from the outside world, other than what the occasional aircraft drops in. How is the war going?"

"It's a struggle," I reply.

"What happened?" she asks.

"It's a long story."

Silence reigns for a moment.

"Omega has resorted to nuclear weaponry," I say at last. "We've lost most of Washington, Oregon and some of California."

Mauve stares at me, then inhales quickly.

"Dear God," she whispers. "My worst fears have been realized."

"I come on behalf of the California militias," I say, "and the National Guard. Commander Chris Young extends his thanks, as well, for welcoming my men and me here in Yukon City."

"We don't get many visitors, these days," Mauve replies, quiet. "At the beginning, we did. We were bringing people in from all over the state. But then, the flow simply stopped. We saved everyone we could save, I suppose. The rest simply perished."

"How long have you been president here?" I ask.

"One year. The people elected me."

"Have you had any issues with Omega? Mercenaries? Rogue elements?"

"No." She pauses. Then, "Well, we've had our issues. But Omega has not penetrated this place. We're very difficult to find, and very small. Some might even say we're not worth their time."

"Some might," I reply. "But what you're doing here is a good thing."

"Indeed it is."

"President Bacardi," I say, leaning forward. "I'm going to be straight with you: I'm not here on vacation. I'm here on a mission."

"I suspected as much." She folds her hands together. "And?"

"I'm here to find reinforcements," I continue. "California is the last thing standing in the way of Omega's total takeover of the West Coast. Right now, Omega views California as valuable enough to preserve it rather than nuking it, and our militia forces are the only thing keeping them from implementing a total takeover."

"So you're here to recruit my men?" she asks.

"I'm here to find volunteers," I reply. "Able-bodied fighting men and women."

"Did it occur to you that perhaps we need those able-bodied fighters here?"

"Yes, but California needs them *more*." I narrow my eyes. "President Bacardi, you live here in peace and solitude. California is a warzone. We need more soldiers, or Omega is going to destroy us, and there will be nothing left of our country."

Mauve considers this. And then she says, "Commander Hart, we're already *fallen*."

"You haven't been out there, in the war," I go on. "I have. I'm telling you, it's brutal. Omega is ruthless – they'll kill anybody who stands in their path. I'm trying to save innocent people from dying."

"People have already died," Mauve responds, flat. "You recruiting more soldiers will change nothing. A dead body can't be brought back to life. Omega overpowers us to such an incredible degree that we have no feasible way to survive. Our best chance at survival is to stay hidden and maintain our own societies, off their radar."

"So you'd rather hide than fight," I say.

Em looks at me, startled by my sarcasm.

"It's a matter of logic, Commander," Mauve replies evenly. "Survival of the smartest, not the fittest."

"There is no such thing as safe," I tell her. "This place is great, but eventually, Omega will find you. If the United States falls completely and the militias are snuffed out...every survivor camp will eventually be located and destroyed. They will show you no mercy."

Mauve taps on the desk.

"Perhaps," she replies.

"I was also told that you possess weaponry here – perhaps nuclear weapons or guns and tanks? We need those, too," I go on.

"We have nothing here for you." Her gaze is cool. "If we did, you would know."

"I'm not sure that I would."

"Trust me, Commander. If you were told that we have weapons like that here, you were either lied to or misinformed. We are a refugee colony, not a fighting colony."

"The presence of the militia and the National Guard makes me think otherwise," I point out. "If you are lying to me, President Bacardi, I will find out."

My threat hangs in the air like an icy current of air.

"You're tired, Commander Hart," she says. Her voice is cold and brittle. "I suggest that you find your quarters and rest. We will discuss this again tomorrow."

I sense the anger – the attitude of stubbornness – rolling off Mauve in heavy waves. I will get nowhere with her today. I stand up. "I'll see you tomorrow, President," I say.

She nods.

Em Davis follows me out of the room, into the hallway.

"Hey," she says.

I look at her.

"I'll help you find your room," she says, jerking her thumb at the stairwell. "Come on."

I move quickly down the hallway with her. The guards are standing along the wall, guarding the president's office. Em, India and myself quickly move around the corner, and step into the stairwell. She climbs quickly – almost erratically – and when we are halfway up the stairs, out of earshot of the guards, she stops.

"I'm sorry," she says breathlessly, shaking her head. "Mauve is...well, she's been through a lot. She considers isolationism our best option. She won't be happy about you recruiting soldiers for the militias in California."

"She doesn't have to be happy about it," I reply. "She just needs to help us."

"Mauve is respected by the people," Em goes on. "When the survivors first started arriving here, a lot of them were sick or dying. Mauve organized the city, made it efficient and safe. They trust her."

"What's your point, Commander Davis?" I demand, agitated.

"My point is that Mauve is a great ally...but she will do anything to keep this place safe and concealed, and what's more, she has the ear of the people. She can turn the people against you in a second." Em leans forward, lowering her voice. "Stay on her good side and you'll have a better chance of finding what you want here."

She starts climbing again.

I take a deep breath and follow. We climb and climb, until we reach the very top – the fourteenth level. It's little more than an apartment floor, long hallways twisting around the structure of the edifice, locked doors and stale, undecorated walls.

"Em," I say.

Em pauses and turns to face me. She looks worried, her eyes rimmed with red.

"I'm not here to hurt anybody," I say. "I'm here to help."

She replies, "I hope you're right."

Elle pops her head out of an open doorway.

"Cassidy," she says. "I mean, Commander. This is sweet!"

I peek inside the room where she's housing with Manny. It's a basic apartment – small kitchen, bathroom, living room and bedroom. A wide, open window overlooks the harbor below. Bravo has his paws on the windowsill, ears perked up, tail wagging.

"Nice," I say.

Elle sits on the couch. It bounces beneath her weight, and she grins. Cheng waltzes in from the bedroom and crosses his arms.

"It seems secure," he mutters. "I don't know that I like being this high up in a building, though."

"Baby," Elle says, making a face.

I keep moving, passing the room where Andrew and Uriah are staying – along with some other men from my detachment. My room is the one on the end. I walk inside to find Vera sitting motionless on the couch, staring out the window. I leave Em Davis in the hall and close the door.

"What is it?" I ask. "Vera? What's wrong?"

She looks at me, exhaling.

"Nothing," she says. "It's just..."

"Spit it out."

"I miss California." She shrugs. "I just miss it."

I sit next to her on the couch.

"Me too," I say.

It's the truth. It's my home, and I miss it, too.

"Any luck with President Bacardi?" she asks.

"No. She denies that they have weapons," I reply.

"Do you believe her?"

"I don't know." I sigh. "And she doesn't want us to recruit."

"I figured."

"I hate to think that this is a dead end mission," I continue.

"You don't know that it is, yet," Vera says.

"Right."

"We'll keep trying. Give it a couple of more days. Maybe the president will warm up to us."

I laugh a little.

"Probably not," I say. "She's not my number one fan."

"Here's a newsflash for you, Cassidy," Vera deadpans. "Not *everybody* is."

Chapter Six

We sleep through the night. I burrow into the bed in the bedroom. It is just me, Vera, Margaret and Isabel here, and I welcome the relative privacy – apart from the rest of the militia. In the early morning, I snap awake, buried under a pile of wool blankets, still fully dressed, my rifle cradled against my arm like a baby.

"Nice hair, ace," Vera remarks, waltzing past my bed. She's wearing a clean set of dark fatigues and a thermal shirt, her hair washed.

"Why are you so clean?" I murmur, annoyed.

"I took a *shower.*" She flicks her platinum-blond hair over her shoulder. "You should do the same – take care of the rat's nest on your head that you like to refer to as *hair.*"

I glare at her, patting my unruly red locks, trying to smooth the curls away.

I slowly roll out of bed, laying my rifle on the blanket. I peer into the living room, dimly lit. Elle and Cheng are sitting on the couch, talking in low tones. Elle is smiling, and Cheng is laughing. Bravo watches the whole thing with a look of curiosity while Manny lounges in the corner, flipping through the pages of a dog-eared book.

"Apparently everybody decided to congregate in our room?" I ask.

"Apparently," Vera replies. "I guess that makes us the popular dorm on campus."

"I guess."

I head toward the bathroom, a simple space with a shower, sink and toilet. I find a pile of clean clothes on the counter with a piece of paper pinned to a green jacket. It reads: *For Commander Hart.* Nice. I peel off my damp clothes and dump them on the floor, shivering in the cold. I step into the shower, elated to discover that there is hot water. I turn the knob and hot water streams out, steaming up the entire room. I beam and step under the waterfall, closing my eyes – thinking.

Can Mauve be trusted? Probably. She seems like a tough, opinionated woman who is clearly used to getting her way. My arrival is probably difficult for her to accept, isolated as she is from the reality of the bloody war with Omega.

We will win this thing. We will.

I get dressed, comb my hair back and watch the slender, strong, sharp-eyed girl in the mirror staring back at me.

Get the job done, I tell myself.

I leave the washroom with a pile of dirty clothes, dumping them under my cot.

Uriah is nowhere to be seen.

"I propose we go find ourselves some breakfast," Manny drawls, standing up. "Who's with me?"

"Count me in," Elle says.

She stands up, leashing Bravo and pulling on her gloves. All of us lace up our shoes and button our jackets, opening the door. We head down the hall. Andrew and Uriah are here, talking. Uriah meets my eyes as I move forward. He stops talking and falls into step with me.

"Chow hall is outside," he says. "Em Davis was here early, and she wanted to make sure you knew where to find it."

"You talked with her?" I ask.

"Yeah."

"What do you think of her?"

Uriah cocks an eyebrow.

"I think she's just as scared as everybody else," he says. "But she knows something."

"Yeah, she warned me to take it easy with President Bacardi," I tell him. "She's giving me resistance about recruiting troops."

"Figures. Nothing is ever easy."

"Nope. Never."

Outside, the morning air is cutting and cold, and the dusky twilight of the winter solstice is disorienting. My men are talking, laughing and hanging out around the Begich Towers, coming and going from a large, white tent erected on the back end of the parking lot. Some of them are smoking cigarettes, and others are playing card games on the steps of the buildings.

I find myself smiling. It is wonderful to see them happy – relaxed, for once.

"Commander Davis told us that they use the old wedding party tent for a mess hall because they ran out of room inside the towers," Andrew tells me, walking hand in hand with Vera. "And get this: before the Collapse, pretty much every citizen in the entire town lived inside the towers. The police department's office was in the bottom level, where President Bacardi is now."

"So the entire city lived under one roof?" Isabel asks. "That's crazy."

"That's how it was."

"That's how it still *is*," Uriah remarks.

We walk inside the massive event tent. Inside, it is glowing with lamplight, and a makeshift buffet table has been set up along the wall. Some of my men are eating at rows of plastic tables, shoveling forkfuls of meat and potatoes into their mouths. It smells wonderful.

There are people I don't recognize, too. Survivors from the campground and city park. They are fairly clean, dressed in basic clothes, keeping their eyes down and their shoulders hunched.

Manny says, "Are these survivors from Yukon City?"

"Yeah."

"Look," Uriah says, gesturing to a sign on the wall. It reads:

Meal Rotation Schedule

0400 Militia

0500 Camp 1

0600 Camp 2

"They got themselves a feeding schedule, nice," Manny remarks. "And where do we fit into this? We missed the 0400 hog-call."

"Davis said we could hit the 0600 this morning," Uriah says. "But tomorrow we need to be dining with the Yukon City militia."

Sounds reasonable.

There is a large group of refugees – maybe fifty – inside the chow hall. They keep to themselves, watching my soldiers with baleful eyes. I get in line with the rest of my platoon. Expressionless women spoon food onto my plate. They avoid eye contact and conversation.

Okay, then. Very friendly.

We find a spot at a table. Just as we are sitting down, a man twists around in his seat, staring at Elle and Bravo.

"Oh, that's a very cute puppy you have there, girly," he says. "Is he for sale?"

Bravo's ears twitch. Elle stands at the table, her fists clenched.

"No," she replies.

Cheng murmurs something to her and touches her arm. She nods, relaxing a bit.

"That's not very polite." The man talking is tall and spindly, with dull gray eyes and a hooked nose. "Don't tell me, the doggy is your friend, right? That's downright adorable."

Laughter.

Suddenly all eyes in the room are on our small table, and I feel like the refugees are looking through us with X-ray vision, whispering amongst themselves. Who are we? Why are we here? Why have we intruded upon their meal rotation schedule?

Elle grips her fork, keeping her back to the man. I know that it is taking everything in her to avoid confronting him, and I applaud her for that. Elle just stands there, staring at the table, her fork in hand. She continues to ignore him, kneeling down and giving Bravo a plate of his own food.

She exhales and relaxes. Good.

The man's eyebrows arch.

"You're giving a *mutt* the food that *we're* supposed to eat?" he screeches. "Hey, look! She's giving *our* rations to a *dog!*"

The ragtag survivors stand at their tables, muttering among themselves. A little girl stands on the table, straining to see, pointing.

Somebody yells, "SELFISH ROTTER!"

Elle looks at me. I take a deep breath.

"No," I warn.

She nods, swallowing.

The man with the hooked nose is clearly an instigator – and he's angry. He stands up, slamming his utensils against the table. They bounce off the plastic and clatter to the ground. The chow hall is now a swirl of yelling and expletives as the refugees stand on their tables or chairs, staring at Bravo, staring at Elle – staring at all of us.

"No dog should get our rations!" somebody yells.

"That's right! EAT THE DOG INSTEAD!"

"KILL THE DOG!"

Elle's eyes widen. I feel a stone drop to the pit of my stomach, sensing what is about to happen. Quicker than a blink, Elle whirls around. She steps onto the table, grabs the man's head and smashes his forehead against the table. He screams, and she drives her fork into his hand, the tongs digging through his flesh and protruding through the palm.

He shrieks in pain, tumbling backward. Elle calmly rolls back over the table, tight, controlled anger flashing in her cool blue eyes. Cheng grabs her arm.

"*No,*" he hisses.

There is a moment of total silence in the room, where everyone – survivors and soldiers alike – are watching the spindly man writhe on the ground, a purple bruise blossoming across his forehead and blood gushing from his hand.

The room explodes.

The ragtag survivors lunge across their tables, headed straight for my platoon and the rest of the soldiers in the chow hall. I jump on top of the table, grabbing the head of one young woman and slamming it against my plate. She goes limp. Elle slides a knife out of her sheath and dances through the assault, driving her blade into an older man's shoulder. He yells, stumbling away, tripping on a bench.

The few soldiers from my detachment meet the force of angry civilians head-on. There is screaming, profanities, confusion. Blood splatters onto the tables and smears across the floor. I see Manny hop on top of a table, swinging a chair by the leg and smacking people in the head. He cackles hysterically, shouting, "Come and get it, you oil-soaked wash rags!"

This is insane. These are civilians. They shouldn't be fighting us. We're protecting them.

I get back to the floor, crushed between civilians and my men. There are only fifteen of my soldiers fighting the fifty or so survivors. But my people are trained to fight – they are conditioned to it. My heart thunders in my chest and the blood pumps through my veins. I spin around Elle, dodging the vicious slash of her knife as Cheng does an impressive flip off the wall, propelling himself into the chest of a huge, burly man with a beard. The man crashes to the ground, dazed. Cheng hops to his feet, a roguish smile on his face. I jump over a fallen survivor and duck a punch by a strong, middle-aged woman with a shaved head. A red, ugly scar cuts up her cheek. She throws another punch. I duck it again, driving my elbow into her neck. She stumbles sideways and I kick her down, where she hits the floor with a dull thud.

I keep moving. Chairs sail through the air, people crash into the plastic tables, shattering or bending them.

Plates careen to the floor, breaking into thousands of pieces. A man with greasy brown hair slides to the ground and picks up a slice of broken glass, clutching it in his hand like a knife. He blocks my path, taking a swing. The tip of the shard slices my shoulder.

I feel a rush of pulsing red fury.

I block his next swipe with my wrist, snapping his hand backward. He screams, and the shard of broken plate falls out of his hand. I jam my knee into his stomach. He careens forward. I spin around, still grasping his arm, and pull his hand backward. His arm cracks, the sound of bone breaking. He screams again, and I let him go. He lands face first on the floor, writhing in pain and shock.

I feel nothing for him.

I look up, sweat running down my face, and see Uriah. I wipe the corner of my mouth with my hand, tasting blood. He flashes through the fight and comes to my side.

"You hurt?" he asks.

"No."

A heavy man wearing a baseball cap tries to grab Uriah from behind, but Uriah is far too agile. He whirls around, trips him, and kicks him into the ground.

I feel a jolt of pride – of power. We are the alpha dogs here. We are the fighters.

As soon as the thought floats through my head, something shatters against the back of my skull. Color explodes before my eyes and I stumble forward, crashing into the glass hood of the buffet counter. The hood crumbles under the weight of my body. Pieces of broken glass dig into the palms of my hand and cut my face. I hit the ground, feeling pain crack through every bone. My head is fuzzy, jarred with pain. Something hot and sticky drips down the back of my neck. Blood?

I struggle to stand, but I am too unsteady. I look up. I see the man with the hooked nose advancing on me. Pieces of a broken plate lay at his feet – and probably in the back of my head, too. He still has a fork embedded in his hand. He lunges toward me, but Uriah grabs him around the neck. He lowers the man to the floor, his face turning a muted shade of purple. I am disoriented – everything is louder than it should be, rushing. I vaguely see the fury in Uriah's black eyes as he steadies his grip around the man's neck. The man kicks and claws, but Uriah is too strong. After a long moment, the man goes still. His limp hand hits the ground, the fork clattering against the concrete floor.

Uriah shoves him aside and rushes to me.

"Cassidy, are you okay?"

I blink.

"Yes," I say. "It just looks bad."

He helps me stand up. And that's when I see it. Leaning against Uriah's body, I see the woman with the shaved head standing in the corner of the room, surveying the chaotic scene around her. She holds a gun in her hand – a small gun, maybe nothing more than a Glock. She lifts it up, gripping it with both hands, until it is even with her chest.

Oh, no you don't.

Pure instinct drives my next movements. I slip Uriah's handgun out of his holster, bring it up, take a breath, aim and squeeze the trigger. The motion is so organic – so fluid – that I do not even have to think about it. It's simply an extension of who I am.

The bullet cracks through the Mess Hall, loud and clear. My aim is spot-on. The woman's head snaps backward, a small, bloody hole blossoming in the center of her forehead. The gun clatters to the floor. She falls to the floor, dead.

Vera sprints across the room and seizes the gun, shoving it into her belt. The refugees freeze, a hush falling over the crowd.

No, no, no. I didn't want to kill her. I didn't want to. But I had to.

The refugees slowly begin to shrink away, and Uriah and I back out of the chow hall. Elle spits on the ground as we exit, her knuckles bloody, a gash above her eye. Bravo follows her closely, his ears down, a fierce growl boiling deep in his throat. Cheng puts his hand on her arm, muttering something that I cannot hear.

"Here comes trouble," Vera says.

A strong detachment of thirty or so National Guard troops screech up to the chow hall in pickups, armed to the teeth. Em gets out of the truck, her gun jammed into her shoulder. Her dog is not here. President Bacardi and her personal detachment of guards flash out of the Begich Towers. She is wrapped in a thick wool coat, towering above most of her men. Her hands are balled into fists.

"What's going on?" Em demands. Weapons are trained on us. All of them.

I hold my bloody hands up.

"Your men confronted us," I say. "We were just defending ourselves."

Em takes a deep breath and nods at a lieutenant on her right. They go inside the chow hall, searching it out. Refugees have begun to disperse as the soldiers arrive, but I hear screaming and wailing from inside the tent.

Em emerges from the tent, her face pale. She whispers something low to Mauve, casting a dark glance at me. Mauve's expression tightens.

"Commander Hart," she says, tightly. "May I have a *word*?"

"Go right ahead," I reply, sharp.

"Pardon my language, Commander," she says, briskly. "But do you mind explaining to me what the *hell* just happened?"

"*You* tell me," I respond.

"One of our civilian refugees is lying dead on the ground, shot right in the center of her forehead!" she says, trembling with rage. "Eighteen others are wounded. Is there a reason for this blatant display of hostility? Because that is *not* something we welcome here, Commander."

She is shaking with rage, looming over me like a dark shadow.

"President Bacardi," I say, surprised by my own sense of calm. "Those so-called refugees threatened to kill a member of my ranks, and one of my soldiers got pushed too far. Those people attacked *us* – not the other way around."

"Really?" President Bacardi raises an eyebrow. "According to the refugees, one of your *people*" – she says the word like it is poison – "stabbed a civilian through the hand with a *fork* after he made a harmless joke about a dog."

"That dog is part of my militia," I say, "and he was threatened. We protect our own."

"Are you telling me that the entire fight inside the hall was started because of a *dog*?" she says, eyes flashing.

"I'm telling you that the fight was started because my men were defending themselves," I reply. "And anybody who threatens us will find themselves dead." I take a step closer to her. "We're fighters, President. We kill people – that's what we do best, remember? So the real question is, why would someone be stupid enough to cross us?"

She stares at me, cold fury burning through her eyes.

"These people are not soldiers," she says. "They're just refugees, trying to stay alive."

"Welcome to the club," I say.

Mauve's lips curl into a hard sneer.

"You will learn how things work here soon enough," she tells me.

I don't reply. I fix her with my coldest glare and move away from the chow hall, back toward the Begich Towers, leaving the mess behind me.

***

I am standing at the window in my quarters, staring over the harbor, when someone raps on the door. Vera is sitting on the couch, and she springs up.

"Visitors," she says. "Great."

She stalks to the door. Both of us are still on edge, barely having washed the blood from the chow hall fiasco off our hands. I watch her open the door. Em Davis stands there, a hard, steely expression on her face.

"May I come in?" she asks.

I nod.

She walks into the room. Vera stands in front of the door, her arms crossed over her chest, ready for a fight. My stance is almost identical – I'm ready to get yelled at again, to get chewed out.

"Commander Hart," Em says. "I'm sorry about what happened this morning."

I raise my eyebrows, surprised.

"I understand why you reacted the way you did," she goes on. "I would have done the same thing, defending my men or my dog."

"Thank you," I say. And I mean it.

"I also came here to warn you," she goes on. "President Bacardi was hesitant to welcome you and your men here in the beginning because of your...*reputation*. What happened today only confirmed her feelings."

"What *feelings*? And what reputation are you referring to?" Vera demands.

"Commander Hart and the Freedom Fighters," Em explains. "You guys have a bit of a rep as hard-hitting, hot-headed fighters. In other words, most militias are afraid of you. They know you're dangerous."

"We're all on the same side here," I say. "Our only enemy is Omega."

"President Bacardi doesn't see it that way. She sees you as usurping her position of leadership." Em shrugs. "She's a strong woman, and she has fought hard to get this city to where it is today. She won't let anybody take it from her."

"That's not what I'm here to do!" I exclaim. "I'm here to look for help, because California is *dying*."

"I understand that, too," Em says, dipping her head. "Which is why I'm here."

I place my hands on the back of the couch.

"President Bacardi might be the resident politician," Em continues, "but I'm still the commanding officer of the Whittier Militia, and I'm making the decision to help you."

"How do you plan to do that?" Vera asks.

A mischievous smile touches her lips.

"Come with me and I'll show you."

Chapter Seven

We leave Begich Towers with Em. Only Vera,
Uriah and myself go with her. Em moves quickly
through the parking lot, her eyes darting back and forth,
her motions tight and controlled. She is nervous – I can
see it, I can feel it. Going up against President Bacardi
must not be something she does very often...if at all.

Her personal pickup is parked on the edge of the
parking lot. I climb into the front passenger seat and
Uriah and Vera get in the back. The windows are icy,
coated with snow. She scrapes it off and then slides
behind the wheel. The engine sputters to life. The heater
struggles to warm the inside of the cab, leaving us to
shiver in the frigid temperature.

"So where are you taking us?" Vera asks.

Em keeps her eyes trained on the road, pulling
out of the parking lot and jolting across the railroad
tracks. "The Roamers," she says. "They'll be able to help
you."

"The Roamers?" I echo. "I thought they were
religious zealots."

"They are. But they're great fighters, always
willing to help kick Omega's butt."

"That's religious enough for me, then."

"It should be." Em smiles slightly. "By the way, if President Bacardi knew I was doing this, she'd probably try to kill me."

"That's nice of her."

"She has no authority over me...not really." Em curls her gloved hands around the steering wheel. "But she has the ear of the people here...she can make anybody's life a living hell, and I need the support of the refugees."

No, I think. *You need the support of the militias.*

"Sounds like President Bacardi's a real pain," Vera says. "Why do the people love her so much if she's such a crackpot?"

"Because she's a *smart* crackpot," Em replies. "And like I said, she brought this place from being harmless Whittier to being the safe zone that is Yukon City."

"What did she do that was so special?" I ask.

We drive parallel to the railroad tracks and speed away from the city park and the towers, running alongside the harbor. The cold, dark water is choppy amidst the slabs of glacial ice bobbing in the bay.

"The whole place was anarchy before she came," Em explains. "Civilians were living here, without any military protection or authoritative guidance. Every kind of person from every different walk of life. Food started to run low and survivors were at each other's throats. Things got ugly – kind of like this morning, but way worse."

"So Mauve was the voice of reason," I guess.

"Yeah," Em replies. "She was that and a whole lot more. She rallied the majority of the camp to her side, and they started organizing the city into sections. She was the architect behind growing crops, even in the dead of winter. We built greenhouses with artificial sunlight, and we've got livestock, too. Medicine, even."

"And when did the militias come into the picture?" I ask.

"About six months ago," Em answers. "Bacardi sent a message to the militias, asking for medicine for our hospital – they were running low on supplies. The militias responded by sending most of what she needed, but they were impressed with this place, so they dug in here too, for the same reason that the United States Military used it as a defense base during the Second World War."

"Because it's hidden," I say.

"Yep, it's practically impossible to find and has defensible perimeters."

"And I'll bet President Bacardi wasn't expecting a military occupation."

"No, I arrived with my militia and the National Guard," Em confirms. "She's been against us since the beginning. Honestly, she can't do anything about us being here. But she has a lot of influence over the people, and if they hate us, they can make our experience here pretty miserable."

I lean back in my seat.

"In the end," I say, "we're still the alpha dogs."

I hear Uriah laugh quietly, and I know that he agrees with my logic.

"I don't disagree," Em says. "I'm just saying: President Bacardi can be difficult to deal with."

We put more and more distance between us and the Begich Towers, until we are approaching the Maynard Tunnel again.

"Whoa, I thought the Roamers were inside the city!" Vera exclaims.

"They're right outside. They like their privacy."

I throw an uneasy glance behind me, at Uriah. My eyes say, *Should we do this?*

He nods, slowly.

Of course we should. This could be a way for us to get help for California.

Em checks in with the guards at the checkpoint, and then we are rolling into the Maynard Tunnel, the darkness closing in around us. I don't like it, but I don't say anything. I can't imagine rolling through this tight, enclosed space for two and a half miles is anyone's idea of a good time.

"I'm glad you came," Em says, "It's good to hear something about the outside world. I was in Camp Pendleton until the militias sent me here. I was with the Marines." Her face tightens. "We had some trouble, some tragedy. I don't know. I was glad to come up here, to escape. But now I wish I was back in the fight."

I turn to her.

"Why do you have to wish?" I ask. "You can help us, too. We need all the fighters we can get."

Em says nothing. Then, "I guess you have a point."

We reach the end of the tunnel, roll through the exit checkpoint and find ourselves back on the other side of the mountains. I love the way that the clouds cling to the peaks, shrouding us in a fairytale-like fantasy.

We keep moving, until the road curves around the back of the mountain, coming to a rock face. It sheers vertically, straight up into the air. The trees on the approaches have been logged, making the landscape dry and barren.

"Welcome to the Roamers' base," Em says.

She pulls the Humvee to the side of the road and I stare at the edifice hacked into the rock mountain, accessible from only one side: the front. It's a fortress – a basic compound, with camouflaged concrete walls and rock barriers around the structure of the central building. The roadway is lined with logs sharpened into spikes. There is one imposing entrance gate, and a maze of concrete barriers and sandbags. I see guns covering us as we roll. Guards are standing out front, clothed in long black coats, with rifles ready.

"This is quite the place," Vera mutters.

"They're quite the people," Em replies.

She turns the Humvee to the left and goes into the maze of blockades, slowly approaching the front gate. The guards must recognize her and her vehicle, because they don't look alarmed as we pull up. Em rolls her window down and the guard walks over. Strange black and white streaks are painted across his face.

"Commander Em Davis," she says. "I'm here with Commander Cassidy Hart, and Lieutenants Vera Wright and Uriah True of the California militias."

The guard peers inside the vehicle, assessing us. He looks at me, raises his eyebrows, and then nods at the other guy standing watch. He steps away, says something into a radio clipped onto his belt, and then the gate opens. First, there is a heavy iron fence, and behind that, a solid barrier made of wood. A cross is painted on the wood, painted with bright orange flames.

It's slightly disturbing, and I try to ignore it.

We roll inside the gates, and I look around. It looks like a compound you might see in the desert – simple, dirty. But this compound is covered with sleet and ice instead of hot desert sand. There are two layers of outdoor hallways. Everywhere, I see men and women alike, wearing long black robes, with heavy rifles or shotguns, many standing along the ramparts, keeping watch.

But every eye is on us as we roll inside.

"Don't worry," Em assures us. "We're allies."

121

"I've heard that line before," Vera mutters.

The Humvee comes to a halt and we exit the vehicle. I'm hyper-aware of the attention we're getting, and I'm glad Em is with us. In the middle of the compound, there is a building dimly glowing from within. A long, stony silence passes.

The front doors – two metal double doors – open, and a woman walks outside. Her hair is white and buzzed short. Behind her, two men follow. They are tall, clad in combat fatigues, heads shaven, and long, draping robes hanging over their clothes. I stare openly, glancing at Uriah. His eyebrows come together, confusion flitting across his face.

Behind them, a large, dark-skinned man emerges from the building. White streaks are painted under his eyes. I take a step back, shocked.

"Father Kareem?" I breathe.

He doesn't smile.

"Cassidy Hart," he replies. "You have returned."

***

"I knew you would find your way to us," Father Kareem says.

I gape, cheeks flushed, shock radiating through my body. I remember this man, clothed in robes, sitting atop a horse, while the grass crackled around us with flames. I was riding my horse, Katana, then, and Uriah was with me.

This man is the leader of the Mad Monks, a fringe group of religious, anti-Omega warriors.

How is this possible?

My mind races with a million hypothetical theories.

"Father Kareem," Uriah echoes. "Your people were in California, in the mountains. What happened?"

Father Kareem bows his head.

"Much has changed," he replies. "It does not surprise me that you have come to us now. The prophecy predicted as much." He waves a hand. "Please, come inside. We will not harm you."

I hesitate – but only for a moment.

We came all the way here to get to this place. I can't back out now.

I walk forward, toward the main building in the dark compound. The woman with the shaved head has striking gray eyes and a slender, upturned nose. "You're the one the prophecy speaks of?" she asks, quietly.

"Um," I reply.

"She is," Father Kareem interjects. "Commander Hart, this is Sister Leslie. She is a friend, and she can be trusted."

Are you *our friend?* I think. *Can* you *be trusted?*

"Commander," Leslie says, folding her hands together and giving a slight bow.

"Father Kareem," Em says, tilting her head respectfully.

"Commander Davis," he replies. "It is good of you to visit with us today."

I glance at Vera. Her brow is knit close together, clearly critical of the situation. But we continue into the building, which is nothing more than a large room with a long, wooden table. The walls are plastered with drawings and maps of Alaskan and Californian terrain, visual records of Omega troop movements and – most bizarrely of all – a portion of the wall is painted with roman numerals. Above the numbers, there are words:

hostium occidit

"Enemy kills," I mutter.

"You speak Latin, Commander Hart?" Father Kareem asks.

"A little," I reply.

He gestures to the long wooden benches paralleling the table. We each take a seat, Commander Em Davis directly across from me, and Vera and Uriah on my right. Father Kareem doesn't sit, he just gazes at us with a searing intensity.

"You did not tell me that the militias were arriving," Father Kareem says to Em at last.

"It was very sudden," Em replies. "They're here on a mission."

"Of course they are," Father Kareem says.

"Father," I interject. "Why are you here, in Whittier? Last time I saw you, you and your men were in California, in the Tehachapi Mountains."

And they were riding horses, no less. How on earth they made the journey from California to Alaska is a mystery to me.

"The religious persecution my people and I suffered at the hands of Omega was too egregious to overlook," Father Kareem replies, calmly. "There were too many deaths, too many executions. We fought ruthlessly against the enemy, but as you know, Commander Hart, there were simply too many. Their numbers were overwhelming, and, slowly, they pushed us backward, taking many of my people prisoner – executing them in public, making examples of them."

A cold chill runs down my spine. Omega is merciless.

"We sought religious asylum with the California militias," he goes on. "They were generous in their help, and we were relocated here, to the snowy wilderness. Here, my people and I have lived in peace, yet we are still able to venture forth and strike deadly blows at our oppressors."

"You're fighting with the militias, then," Vera says

"We are."

I look at Father Kareem, tall and stately; dark and dangerous. The leader of the Mad Monks, and now the leader of the Roamers. How it is that our paths crossed, I don't know, but there must be a reason.

"Father Kareem," I say. "I'm here on behalf of the California militias. I don't know how long it's been since you've been in California, but things are looking bad. Omega has dropped nuclear weapons on Washington, Oregon, Canada and part of California. They just took over San Francisco, and they're pushing their way into the Central Valley." I look him straight in the eye. "I'm not just here to hide out. I'm here on a mission. We need reinforcements and weapons, and we need them bad."

"It is not possible to overpower Omega with sheer manpower," Father Kareem replies. "Their foot army is too vast – hundreds of thousands, if not millions, comprise their ranks."

"We need more fighters," I say. "More sharp minds. We need all the help we can get, and I don't care where it comes from."

"You are here to ask me if I am willing to offer my people as your allies in this final stand against the enemy," Father Kareem observes. "You are desperate; I can see that in your eyes. It is as I believed it would be."

Uriah's face is fixed into one of stern annoyance – he's not religious and the Mad Monks have never been his favorite people. Vera, on the other hand, is expressionless.

"We're all in this together," I say, sighing. "If the world falls, we fall with it. Omega has killed so many of us already – friends, family. They've taken away everything, but we can still stop them. It might not be easy – and we might die in the process. But we can do it. We have something they don't: motivation. We want victory more than they do, because this is our *home*."

"I know this, Commander," Father Kareem answers, slowly. "My people have been persecuted more than yours have – we have indeed both suffered greatly." He turns around, his hands clasped behind his back. The woman with the white hair regards us with a cool, calm gaze as he stares at a mural on the wall: it looks fairly new, a painting of a black cross twisted with thorns, and around the base, fire is burning all around it.

"The world is in a dangerous and precarious position, young soldier," Father Kareem goes on. "We are on the precipice of destruction, in its most ungodly and blackened form. We are all that stands between the earth and total annihilation."

"Nuclear war," I whisper.

"Indeed. A war of fire and ash."

"It's impossible," Sister Leslie suddenly says. Her eyes – and her voice – are stone cold. "We cannot outmatch or overpower the enemy. Not with sheer brute force. We simply don't have enough manpower."

She seems desperate to convey this to Father Kareem, fixing me with a tense glare.

"Sister Leslie speaks the truth," Father Kareem agrees. "If we keep fighting, it will be a fight to the death. They will overcome us all."

For a long while, nobody speaks.

"But," Father Kareem says at last, "I would not be a true man of the Holy God and neither would my people if we simply denied help to those who ask us to come to their aid." He looks at me, an ever-so-slight smile tugging on the corners of his mouth. "My people and I will help you, Commander Hart, but there are conditions."

My heart does a back flip, stunned. This...this is wonderful.

Reinforcements at last!

"What are your conditions?" I ask, keeping my expression calm.

"Father," Sister Leslie says, "we have been doing incredibly well here in Alaska, attacking the enemy from our winter fortress. Leaving will kill us all, and we –"

Father Kareem holds up a hand, and she immediately falls silent.

"We will do this," he says. "And that is the last we will speak of it."

Sister Leslie bows her head, her jaw clenched. She glares at me again, then crosses herself and looks at the mural on the wall, refusing to face the rest of the people in the room.

Em Davis looks at me, her face grave. She slowly shakes her head, as if trying to convey some secret message to me. I raise an eyebrow but say nothing, turning back to Father Kareem.

"My conditions are simple," Father Kareem replies. "Total transparency, and of course my men will ultimately answer to me, not the militias."

"Of course," I agree.

"Commander, you and your men have a reputation; Angels of Death, I believe they call you," he goes on. "It is an apt nickname. If you help my men strike a deadly blow at the enemy here in Alaska, we will go wherever you want us to go, and we will gladly fight by your side until this war is over."

Em closes her eyes, shaking her head.

"What do you want us to do?" I ask.

"Fulfill the prophecy," he replies.

Chapter Eight

A hush falls over the room. The Mad Monks' prophecy regarding the apocalypse and a certain girl with "flaming" hair has long been a running joke in the militia ranks. No one takes it seriously, but here, in the room with Father Kareem, I am suddenly afraid of what he's about to say.

"What prophecy?" I ask, hesitant.

"You fear religion," Father Kareem replies, raising one eyebrow. "You fear it because you cannot grasp it, and yet it is shaping you even now, as we speak."

"I don't understand," I say.

"I foresaw this apocalypse long before it ever happened," he goes on. "And I am not the only one who predicted it. The Holy God gave me a vision, along with several others, of our saving grace, and I know only that you will have a part to play in it." He shrugs. "Perhaps your work here will fulfill the prophecy."

"What do you want us to do?" I ask.

"Sister Leslie," Father Kareem says. "Bring the map."

Sister Leslie scurries to the far end of the room, peeling a map off the wall, then laying it flat against the table. We stand up and gather around it. I see a map of the lower southern coast of Alaska, reaching into the coastline of Canada.

Near Juneau, there is a red marker circling a white spot.

"What is it?" Uriah asks, flashing a dark look at Father Kareem.

"The enemy," Father Kareem replies. "Omega has taken over Juneau, but they are harboring a secret military base at Mendenhall Lake, miles away from the actual city."

"What kind of a base are we talking about?" I ask.

"It's a defense base," Sister Leslie answers, her words clipped. "It's small, but it's heavily stocked with Omega weaponry – guns, vehicles, tanks and rockets. A detachment of maybe two hundred Omega soldiers are stationed there at all times, guarding it."

I feel a shiver of excitement – only two hundred men standing guard?

Piece of cake.

"So they're just guarding their compound?" Vera asks.

"They're guarding their compound *and* their weaponry," Father Kareem tells us. "And it is quite a considerable amount of goods. Our intel suggests that Omega has more than mere tanks and guns stocked here – possibly something more dangerous."

"Like what?" I ask.

"I suppose that is the question that cannot be answered until we get inside, but we theorize that they may have valuable intel that could greatly aid our cause."

"You just want us to infiltrate the base?"

"I want *us* to infiltrate the base," he corrects. "And kill every breathing Omega soldier inside, and seize their weapons, vehicles, aircraft and computers. Commander, I want our forces to take their base and make it ours."

A military occupation.

I think about this for a moment – what an incredible goldmine this would be. It could change the game for us: access to their weapons, their aircraft, and a peek into their top secret computer databases. Imagine the kind of stuff we could dig up on Omega – locations of secret bases, supply drops, troop deployments...everything!

"Why us?" I prod. "Why haven't you made a move on this place before? You've got a sizable force of men at your disposable – and Commander Davis has a fairly big detachment of men."

"I have been waiting for the opportune moment," Father Kareem says. "And you, Commander, are it. I believe you and your men have been in enough tight spots to understand that what I need for this mission is experience – and lots of it. The National Guard here...their hearts are pure, but they are lacking the skills that I need to make this mission a success."

I get it. He wants seasoned vets to fight against Omega. I'd want the same.

I look at Em.

"You seem distressed," I say, gauging her pained expression. "Spill."

"It's just logistics," Em replies, shooting a pointed look at Father Kareem. "This locale is extremely dangerous; the guards there aren't just your run-of-the-mill Omega soldiers. They're *Elites*, essentially Omega's Special Forces. They're dangerous – well trained, and two hundred of them isn't just a walk in the park."

I consider this.

"Have you ever tried attacking them before?" I ask.

"No."

"Then we have the element of surprise on your side. That's good."

"Mendenhall Base is a suicide mission," Em snorts. "I won't send my men in there."

"Okay," I say, shrugging. "Nobody's asking you to. This is a deal between Father Kareem and my men. Nobody else."

She looks surprised, then shifts her gaze to the table.

"Will you do this?" Father Kareem asks. "Are you willing?"

I glance at Uriah. His firm, steady gaze tells me what I need to know.

"Yes," I say. "We're all in."

***

My hands are slicked with sweat as I stand in the meeting room, staring at the fiery cross on the wall. Elle, Bravo, Cheng, Manny, Andrew and the rest of my detachment slowly filter inside. Many of the men here comprise the Angels of Death, my personal strike team – the same team that completed the dangerous HALO jump into the Kings Canyon in California, into the heart of enemy territory.

These guys aren't just fighters. They're the definition of fearless.

Elle keeps Bravo close to her knee as they sit, Cheng sliding into place beside her, his eyes trained on the map on the table. I am not nervous about presenting the idea of another mission to them; no, that is not what frightens me. What scares the living daylights out of me is the knowledge that there is a very real chance that most of the people in this room – including the ones I love and care about the most – may not make it back alive.

And that is the most terrifying part of this war: the threat of loss. I can see the bewilderment on Manny and Andrew's faces as they come inside, faced with Father Kareem, the legendary leader of the Mad Monks. They are just as shocked as I was an hour ago, wondering how on earth we crossed paths again…how this all happened.

Maybe Father Kareem is right, and this is all part of a greater plan.

"Good morning, ladies and gentlemen," I say, folding my arms across my chest. "You're here today because Father Kareem and his men have made us an offer that I have accepted. Reinforcements in return for our aid on an attack on Omega."

There are some low murmurs – some laughter. I know what they are thinking: *Easy. A walk in the park. No problem. We can max this mission in an hour.*

"I want it to be made perfectly clear that this is a volunteer mission," I say. "It's very dangerous – different than anything we've ever done before. We'll be tackling Omega Special Forces on their turf, and seizing their assets, establishing an occupation in their base. If anyone here wants out, let me know right now, because there's no turning back."

The room is stone silent.

"Good," I say. "Our mission codename is Glacier, and our target is this place right here." I place my hand on the map. "Mendenhall Base. It's a lake, and we're going to kill the Special Forces there and take everything they have. And I do mean everything, guys. We're seizing their aircraft, their vehicles, their weaponry, their intel. Everything."

I see some smiles, hear some excited dialogue. This is a big deal. All this time, we've been on the defensive, hiding from Omega and hitting back at them. This mission is different. We'll be dealing out the punishment, taking *their* stuff, and best of all...we're getting reinforcements out of it, along with an occupied military base. We'll be on offensive for once.

"How are we going in?" Elle asks.

"We'll come in by air six klicks behind enemy lines," I reply. "And then we'll continue to the base on foot."

Father Kareem sets another map on the table, one I've never seen before.

"The base is heavily guarded on three sides, and the waterfront is overlooked," Father Kareem says. "The reason is simple: they have a large lookout tower on the island in the middle of the lake – it's their communications building."

"But we've found a hole," I say. I press my finger against the front of the compound, etched onto the map. "There are large drainage pipes running underneath the base, and we can infiltrate the compound by using these pipes as an entrance point. We'll scale the sides of the building and get inside. Once there, we'll separate and systematically take our platoons through the building, taking down anybody who gets in our way." I take a step back. "No mercy. Understood?"

There are murmurs of, "Yes, Commander."

"What about the communications island?" Manny asks.

"We're going to take them out by using their own weapons on them," I reply.

"Indeed," Father Kareem agrees. "Once we seize the base, taking the island should be simple. Air support will arrive from Yukon City after we have taken the compound and killed the Elites. Blackhawks will cover the island and make sure Omega does not evacuate their communications buildings. We will not only take the island, but we will take the intel workers there hostage."

"How many Special Forces are we looking at?" Andrew asks.

"Two hundred, give or take," Father Kareem answers. "Your detachment is thirty fighters, and mine is fifty."

"Risky odds," Vera mutters.

"We'll be fine," I assure her. "We're better than they are."

She doesn't seem so sure, but she doesn't verbalize her doubts – just like I don't verbalize mine. We have to stay positive, after all. It takes me another hour to finish the details and assignments for the mission.

"Any questions?" I ask, looking around the room of hardened faces.

Cheng says, "This move will either be the smartest thing we've ever done or the most dangerous. Omega will be infuriated if we take a base like this from them – *Veronica Klaus* will be infuriated."

"Good," I say. "They need to be put on the defensive for once."

"They may retaliate with another nuclear attack," Cheng replies.

I exhale.

"We're fighting for our lives," I tell him. "This is something we're doing, because we have no other choice, and because we need the reinforcements and weapons in California."

"Father Kareem and his men will return with us to California to join the Freedom Fighters when this is over," I say. "And we will take the Omegan weapons that we seize with us."

"Wow, this really *is* a big mission," Andrew remarks. "This is bigger than anything we've ever done before – this could really help California."

"Yes," I say. "That's why we have to do it."

There are no arguments.

"We move out at 0400," I say. "Get your rest, eat up. We'll rendezvous at Begich Towers and rally from that point onward. Understood?"

"Yes, Commander," they echo.

"You're dismissed."

They rise from their seats, talking quietly among themselves. My personal lieutenants, including Uriah and Vera, hang back to talk with me.

"So what if we get there and we're outnumbered?" Vera asks. "What do we do? Where do we run? There's nowhere to run *to*."

"We'll have an RV point in case of a retreat," I reply. "Alaska is the perfect terrain for us, Vera. It's a lot like fighting in California, guerilla-warfare style. That's our expertise, remember?"

She sighs. "Yeah. I remember."

"We can do this."

"Indeed," Father Kareem interjects. "God will guide us. We will be victorious."

Vera looks at me and rolls her eyes, whisking away with Andrew in tow. Uriah remains at the table with me, along with Elle and Cheng.

"So we'll be able to bring back reinforcements," Elle says. "Plus enemy weapons and seized enemy intel. I think this is a good mission – a great one."

"If we survive," Cheng replies, darkly.

Father Kareem places a hand on my shoulder.

"We will," he says. "If God is willing, the vengeance of the persecuted will be swift and powerful."

I'm not sure what I think about Father Kareem's violent take on religion, but I don't care. All I know is that we're finally getting something that we want, and I'm willing to take this risk to achieve it.

"0400," I say again. "Be ready."

Father Kareem nods.

I head with Uriah outside, into the dark compound. All around me, the Mad Monks – or the Roamers, as the people of Yukon City call them – are silently watching us. They are like their leader, solemn and silent. I notice Sister Leslie standing in the shadows, the hood of her dark robe pulled over her bare scalp.

She is watching me with a piercing gaze. I don't like it, so I look away, mentally noting to keep an eye on her in the future.

"Cassidy," Uriah says quietly.

"Yeah?"

"You really think we can do this? Omega Special Forces aren't anything any of these guys have been up against before."

"We *are* the militia's Special Forces," I say. "This isn't anything we can't handle."

"I know."

"But you're doubting. Because Chris isn't here."

Uriah shrugs. "He's a SEAL. This is his expertise."

"You don't think I should be leading this mission?"

Uriah stops and looks at me, long and hard.

"I didn't say that," he tells me at last. "I just think this is dangerous."

"Give me one scenario so far in this war that hasn't been dangerous," I snap. "This is *war*. We fight to the *death*."

"I'm not questioning your leadership, Cassie," Uriah says, quietly. "I didn't mean it like that. You know that I'd die for you."

I see a flash of raw emotion in his dark eyes, and I feel a lump in my throat.

"Don't die for me," I tell him, sharp. "Die for something bigger than that."

I don't speak to him again until we leave the compound.

Chapter Nine

We return to Begich Towers for the night. When we arrive, pulling up in our small convoy, the icy air kissing our faces, there is a commotion outside the building. Civilian refugees are gathered at the base of the edifice – children are holding makeshift signs that read: "MILITIAS KILL" and "JUSTICE FOR CLAUDIA."

I knit my brow and slowly approach the gathering of people blocking the doorway to the building. Uriah and Vera fall into step beside me, with Andrew, Elle, Cheng, Manny and Bravo taking up the rear. The Angels of Death emerge from their vehicles, too, wary of the situation.

I don't see Em Davis or Mauve Bacardi anywhere.

The fun never stops, I think.

"...We demand justice!" someone is yelling.

I step into open space between my men and the civilians – maybe fifty at the most. A man with a curly beard and beady black eyes is holding a large rock in his hand. He is flushed and red. The people behind him are fuming.

"THERE SHE IS!" he yells. "THAT'S THE WOMAN WHO SHOT CLAUDIA!"

Angry shouts. Yelling. I keep my face calm and expressionless.

"ENOUGH!" I shout.

"Your people killed our people!" the man with the curly beard exclaims, eyes flashing. "You think that we're going to let you get away with that?"

"Your people were trying to *kill* my men," I reply, leveling my gaze. "Soldiers. Militiamen. Fighters. They were defending themselves."

"You killed my *daughter!*" he hisses. Tears glimmer in his eyes.

I feel a stab of guilt, but I remember how the girl was holding a gun, intending to kill my men – she could have killed Elle, or Manny. Or Uriah.

And then the guilt is gone, replaced by white-hot anger.

"We're fighting for you," I tell him. "Don't get in our way or we will *move* you out of the way."

149

"We don't want your help, you bloody murderers," the man hisses. "Yukon City was better off before your bloodthirsty lot came along."

Uriah tenses beside me, his finger hovering over the trigger of his rifle.

Elle takes a step forward, standing beside me.

"This isn't worth it," she says. "All of this fighting. *I'm* the one who started the fight in the chow hall. I was threatened, so I took action. I'm sorry about what happened, but you guys are too sheltered. We've been *out* there, being killed by Omega. We're not going to take bullying or threats from anyone. Understand that and respect that and we'll be fine."

She locks eyes with me.

This is her apology for starting the fight – for losing control.

I nod. It's okay.

The man with the curly beard glares at me.

"You cannot atone for the death of my daughter – or the death of our people," he growls. "You must stand trial before the senate."

I lick my lips and turn my gaze to Uriah. He gives me a *look.*

"Get out of our way," I say. "We're going inside."

I think about how late it is – and how little time we have to sleep before we rendezvous at 0400 for Operation Glacier. I don't have time for this crap.

But this could get messy.

As if to validate my thoughts, I hear the slide and lock of guns, rounds sliding into chambers and I see knives slipping out of their sheaths. I can feel the crackling tension and the rising adrenaline in my men behind me. And I know, without a doubt, that if a fight starts, there will be no stopping it, and these people will die. It will be a bloodbath, and that is not something I am interested in starting.

"We're not going to fight you," I say, holding my hand up, stilling my men.

The man with the beard raises his right hand, his fingers curled around the rock. He pulls back, as if to hurl it straight at my head. Uriah raises his rifle into his shoulder, ready to take the shot – protecting me, as always.

"No!"

A young boy steps forward, out of the crowd of civilians. He places his hand on the arm of the man ready to throw the rock.

"You can't do it, papa," he says. "She's right. No more killing...*please.*"

The boy looks around twelve years old. His hair is shaved to the scalp. He is dirty, his face smudged with grease. The bearded man slowly lowers the rock, taking several deep breaths and then placing his hand on the boy's shoulder.

He glares at me, his lip quivering.

One second. Five seconds. Fifteen seconds.

He looks up at me. He drops the rock.

"This isn't over," he says, teeth grinding together.

I don't reply.

We slowly work our way to the door of the Begich Towers, as the civilians part around us, the tension fizzling out like a dead breeze. My men move inside, but I stand there, watching, waiting for something to happen. But the man eventually moves on, taking the small, wise boy with him. And pretty soon we are left alone, and it is just Elle, Bravo and me in the parking lot.

"I'm sorry about this," she says, quietly. "It's my fault."

"It is what it is," I reply. "Don't be sorry."

"I don't know why they hate us so much."

152

"They're threatened by us."

"I guess."

We move inside the building. At the far end of the hall, standing in the shadows with her guards, is President Bacardi, her arms crossed over her chest, and her face arranged into a cold glare.

Most of my men have dispersed into the upper levels of the building, exhausted and eager to sleep. Only Uriah remains below, along with Elle and Bravo. The door clangs shut behind me and we are trapped inside with the guards and Mauve.

"Commander Hart," Mauve says. "We need to talk."

"Negative," I reply. "I have a busy day tomorrow, and I need to rest. It can wait."

"It cannot. This needs to be discussed *now*."

Will this night ever end? I think.

"Okay," I say. And then I look at Uriah, silently telling him with my eyes to come with me. So he does. He follows me into Mauve's large, spacious office on the bottom level, while Elle and Bravo hang back in the hall. The office doors shut behind us, and Mauve keeps her back to us for a long moment, staring at the wall. At last, after a heavy silence, she turns to me, her forehead wrinkled in thought.

"Your presence here has upset the refugees," she says, simply. "And honestly, Commander Hart, I am willing to overlook that, because I understand that these things just *happen* sometimes." Her eyes narrow. "But I am *not* willing to overlook your alliance with the Roamers."

"Does our alliance bother you?" I ask.

"That's a nice way of saying it." She stalks to her desk, throws a map down and glares at me. "The Roamers are the best protection we have outside of Yukon City. They guard the Maynard Tunnel, and keep our location secret."

"The Roamers are independent," I reply. "They do what they want, when they want. They're dangerous, and we're going to help them strike back at Omega."

"And in turn, take them away from protecting this city," she hisses.

"You have the National Guard *and* the militias here!" I exclaims. "You don't need the Roamers."

"The Roamers are *deadly*," she says. "We are safer with them here."

"Don't get greedy," I answer, calm. "This is a war, and you and your people in Yukon City are living in a bubble. Everywhere else, Omega has unleashed hell. We need every available fighting man and woman now. This is the final stand."

"You don't understand what it's like up here," Mauve goes on, almost as if I didn't say anything. "It's isolated, freezing, dark...nobody cares about us up here. It's barren and cold. I hate it here, Commander. And so does everybody else."

"I don't know what to tell you," I say, simply. "You and your people are living in luxury compared to the rest of the world – you should be grateful." I pause. "We're deploying tomorrow at 0400. Accept it." I hold up one finger. "I'm sorry it has to be this way."

But I'm not really sorry. I may be a senator for the Pacific Northwest Alliance – which, by the way, may or may not still exist – but I am not going to play a game of politics with a stubborn, paranoid president.

Not today.

I turn on my heel and exit the room, Uriah ghosting along beside me.

"You will be sorry you did this to us," Mauve says, her eyes wild.

155

I ignore her. We leave the room and enter the hallway, keeping quiet until we are past the guards and climbing the stairwell.

"I've had enough drama for one day, haven't you?" Uriah whispers.

I release a breath I hadn't realized I'd been holding.

"Yeah," I say. "Plenty."

***

Operation Glacier

0400

In the forest, I am home. Even in the dark twilight of the Alaskan winter, with the snow crunching beneath my boots, I feel calm. The cloak of nature is my refuge, and I know how to use it to my advantage. It is one of few upper hands I have against the enemy.

The trees are tall, sinister shadows around us as we ghost through the woods. Father Kareem and the Mad Monks move ahead of us, their dark cloaks twisting into the shadows. Tiny flurries of snow pelt my uniform. The air is numbingly cold, different than the cold of the Kings Canyon or the Central Valley in winter. This is an ancient, deep freeze. It's as awe-inspiring as it is annoying.

My rifle is strapped across my back, and the rest of my gear is fairly light. I don't want to be burdened down with heavy equipment when we reach the base – I will need to move quickly and silently. Nothing bulky can be allowed to slow me down.

We keep a steady pace through the woods, the radio piece in my ear silent. The terrain of the mountains begins to slope downhill, and I know that we are getting closer to our destination – but, since we are buried within thick trees, I can't see the lake yet.

At last, Father Kareem's voice crackles into the earpiece: "Hold."

I slide to a halt and place my hand on the trunk of a tree, catching my breath. Uriah is directly behind me, and Vera and Andrew are on my left. Elle is up ahead with Manny and the Mad Monks, using Bravo to clear the path before us in case of booby traps or landmines.

"Yankee Leader," Manny says. "This is Sundog. We have visual on the target."

I close my eyes, inhaling. Exhaling.

"Copy that, Sundog. Team Leaders, assume your strike positions."

My platoon gathers around me, and the rest of the Angels of Death do the same, divided into three small platoons – each one with a designated leader. The first platoon is mine, the second is Vera's and the third is Manny's. Uriah is the best shooter in the entire detachment, so he stays with me. Father Kareem and his men are separate from our detachments and are commanded by him.

"Let's rock and roll," Uriah whispers.

I nod, and then we are moving through the woods again, coming to the bottom of the hill, to a small clearing of trees. Father Kareem and the monks are gathered here in a crouch, behind a berm of earth, staring directly ahead.

Before us lies the Mendenhall Lake, flat and delicate amidst the snowy mountains. Sheets of sharp, papery ice skid across the surface of the water. Occasional glaciers poke out of the lake, too, blue and cobalt, dusted with snow. To our right, a frozen waterfall stretches into the lake, crystalline and impressive. And in the far corner of the lake, I see the Mendenhall Glacier. It's massive, rising out of the ground and curving away between the mountains, a solid, mountainous river of blue ice. It is a massive, icy kingdom, looming and unconquerable. Its sheer size is staggering – over thirteen miles long and hundreds of feet high. It looks like a mammoth river that suddenly froze solid, leaving a stretched, ebbing trail of ice in its wake.

Now that I think about it, that's probably *exactly* what happened.

"Unbe-freaking-lievable," Uriah mutters. "Ever see anything like it?"

"No," I reply. "Not even close."

"It makes Kings Canyon look small."

My eyes are drawn to a clearing across the lake, near our position. There is an open area marked "photo point." And beyond that, a trail that leads back to a small collection of buildings.

"That's the Visitor Center," Father Kareem tells me, his voice quiet. "Omega has brought in more temporary buildings around the area."

I see a parking lot packed with Omega vehicles, once reserved for tourists who were visiting the mighty Alaskan frontier. Everywhere, there are makeshift barracks comprised of temporary buildings – similar to mobile homes, only all of them are painted gray, and stamped with a black O, signifying Omega's domain. Erected on the edge of the mainland, there is a huge building, clearly meant to be an impenetrable compound. It towers four stories into the air, guarded by Omega soldiers. The Omega flag flutters in the cold breeze, hanging from a pole in front of the compound: a black square with an insidious white O in the center, an all-seeing eye.

I scan the entire base quickly – the compound, a tall, dangerous fortress on the edge of the lake, and the rest of the encampment...little more than a collection of barracks, vehicles and a chow hall, which was previously a tourist visitor center.

It is almost 0600, and I can see very dim lights coming from within the chow hall. The main compound, however, is as dark as a tomb – as is the rest of the entire camp.

We stay silent and still for a moment, overlooking everything, making sure we're not walking into some kind of obvious trap. But there is nothing I can see that is out of place – it is exactly as we thought it would be.

"This is Yankee Leader," I say into the radio. "We have a green light."

And we move out in formation, slipping down the side of the mountain, toward the backside of the *Nugget Falls Trail*.

The trail that winds through the rocky soil, away from the trees, is elevated on a berm of earth. Below it, there are three large, iron grates. Behind those grates are the drainage pipes that lead to the far side of the Omega compound.

My team approaches them swiftly, and as we had hoped, they are old and outdated. They easily come off, and my men lay them aside. I take a deep, shuddering breath, bump fists with Uriah, and then he and I, along with Father Kareem, dive into the first tunnel on the left. Vera's platoon takes the middle pipe, and Manny's takes the one of the far right. I flip on the flashlight mounted on my rifle, beaming a sharp path through the grimy tunnel. The ground is slick with slushy ice and mud, and the smell of rot is strong. I tell myself not to think about it – to keep moving.

So we do. The pipes are big enough that I can stand upright, but Uriah has to hunch over slightly. I guess I'm just fortunate to be short today. We keep going for what seems like an eternity, never daring to speak aloud or breathe too raggedly, afraid that the noise will alert Omega to our presence.

I feel a burst of cold air on my face, and I know that we have reached the end of the tunnel. I see the dim twilight of the outside, and I come to a halt at the end of the tunnel. Under normal circumstances, these pipes would be dumping water into the lake, but right now, they are empty, and we halt to gaze at the frozen water below us. I make a fist and bring two fingers to my lips, straining for sounds. I hear the distant whine and rumble of a generator, and the slamming of car doors. But other than that, I hear nothing.

Good. Here we go.

Father Kareem, Uriah and I step to the very precipice of the tunnel and remove the grappling hook guns from our belts. We aim them at the edge of the compound towering above us. The walls are made of concrete, reminding me of a compound that you might see in Afghanistan or Iraq – all flat edges and dirt-colored walls. I feel like I'm staring up at an impenetrable castle of darkness, like the knight in every fairytale, trying to rescue a damsel in distress...only there is no damsel. Just a mission. I squeeze the trigger and the cable launches out of the chamber of the gun with a *thump, swish* and *whir* of the uncoiling line. It disappears from sight, but I hear a faint *thud-clang* as the grappling hook grasps the side of the wall. I pull on the line. It goes taut.

I sling my rifle over my shoulder and test my weight on the line. I look at Uriah, who is little more than a dark shadow in this light. He nods, squeezes my shoulder, and then I begin to climb, my gloves giving me a good grip. It takes every ounce of muscle and upper-body strength that I have acquired over the last two years to make this climb, my boots wedged against the wall, my legs pushing me upward, my arms and shoulders burning with the strain. The *whoosh* of the rest of the grappling hooks deploying distracts me – but only for a moment. I concentrate on the task at hand.

If I fall, I'm dead. So don't look down, don't think. Just do.

I move up, biceps straining, shoulders screaming for relief.

Just a few more feet. Please let me make it.

The terror of failure is enough of a motivation to get me to the top. I barely hook my arm over the edge of the wall and swing my body up, rolling over the ledge. I hit the ground, thanking God that I didn't screw up the climb and plummet to my death, and then I pull myself together.

I crouch on one knee, pulling my rifle into my shoulder. We're standing on the roof of the compound, with nothing but wires and satellite dishes to herald our arrival. I exhale, relieved, and wait for the rest of the men to make it to the top. Father Kareem lands gracefully on his feet – unlike me, the queen of face-plants – and Uriah is right behind him. I see Manny and his platoon, along with Vera. Elle has remained in the pipes with a small detachment of Mad Monks, guarding the entrance to the tunnels.

"Stage one complete," Uriah says into the radio. "Let's go, stage two."

My snipers – and Father Kareem's snipers – take positions along the rooftops of the compound, lying prone and making nests for themselves on the edge. Below, the entire camp lies below us.

I feel alive, invigorated.

We are doing good, so far. We need to keep it up.

On the roof, there is a door that leads to the interior of the compound. This is the most dangerous part – the entrance inside, the knowledge that we are walking into a building filled with dozens of Omega Special Forces.

We pause at the door, gathering around it. Vera's steely blue eyes flash through the slit in her balaclava. "Let's do this," she says.

Father Kareem crosses himself, then checks his heavy rifle one last time.

"God be with us," he says softly.

Ditto, I think.

Uriah takes the primary position and I stay just behind his shoulder. I feel a pang of loneliness, knowing that if Chris was here, I would be staying behind *his* shoulder. But I remind myself that what we are doing here tonight will bring me back to Chris, and then the flash of sorrow is gone.

For now.

Uriah shoves the muzzle of his shotgun into the handle of the door, a forty-five degree angle in, and a forty-five degree angle out. He looks at me – his cover man – and I nod. He shoots. He kicks the door open, and I move inside.

We're in.

***

The first thing that I notice about Mendenhall Base is the darkness. The halls barely glow with dim lighting, and as I make my entrance inside, clearing the first corner, the floors are simple and bare, my boots squeaking on the surface.

My chest constricts and my adrenaline spikes, going straight into the belly of the beast like this. We have been inside enemy bases before...but nothing this big, this obvious. I swallow my fear and keep moving. My team keeps tight and controlled behind me. Father Kareem's men are silent and stealthy – they keep up with us, perfectly trained. I am grateful for their presence here.

We are not fighting alone.

The hallway curves to the left, and I see a row of office doors and beyond that, a simple stairwell leading down to the bottom level. It is eerily silent. I make a note of the quiet and move forward, controlling my breathing.

What would we do if someone came around the corner right now?

Simple: you'd shoot them. Duh.

I don't see any cameras in the hallway – thank God – and as we ghost past the office doors, I am grateful that every single one is closed. I still don't see any sign of movement. Apparently this level is closed for now, which is a major plus for my strike team.

I clear the stairwell and start moving down, Father Kareem and his men covering our advance. Below, I see the glow of white light, and I hear the distant murmur of voices.

Ah, here we are.

I move quickly and silently onto the third level. Here, one office door is standing open, leading to a large room full of small cubicles. I press my shoulder against the wall and peer inside. Men and women alike are sitting at small desks, typing away at computers, their eyes glued to the screen. They are all dressed in dark blue uniforms. Many of them are Chinese, although I spot some Russians and Arabs among the group, as well.

It will be impossible to continue down the hall without one of us being seen. We will have to take the third level, and leave some of our men to take the office workers hostage. I will have to –

A woman comes around the corner. Her short black hair is pulled into a tight bun. She is grasping a mug of coffee. She sees us – all thirty-five of us – and shrieks. Her mug hits the floor and shatters, and she stumbles back into the office. The workers inside blink out of their electronic daze, startled.

No choice, then? Okay.

I enter the room, and my men pour in behind me. The office workers scream and shriek, stumbling away from their desks. One enterprising young Chinese man grabs a handgun from the drawer of his desk. I shoot him before he can pull the trigger. The woman with the tight bun screams again, falling to her knees.

"All right," I say into the radio. "Backup will be on the way. Proceed according to plan."

"Roger that, Yankee Leader," Uriah's voice answers.

"It will be done," Father Kareem replies.

Out of the corner of my eye, I see Manny sweep into the room, taking a position by the door. Father Kareem and his men move quickly into the office, corralling the office workers into a corner at gunpoint. There is a lot of crying, a lot of begging – a lot of people getting down on their knees and chattering frantically in languages that I do not understand.

Ten Mad Monks station themselves in the room, hiding behind desks and the corners of the walls. Uriah and I, along with Vera's platoon, disperse into the hallway. A red light has begun to flash in the corners of the ceilings. I figure this is because somebody activated a panic button at their desk, but it's not a big deal. This is part of the plan. We can deal with it.

Vera nods at me and leads her platoon into the top level of the compound, and I take my men and we enter the door on the right of the hallway. This is an empty office room, dark and lifeless. We flash inside, taking positions behind desks and cubicles, allowing the darkness to envelope us as we crouch low, waiting for our cue. It doesn't take longer than thirty seconds for the Omega response team to show up. They barrel up the stairwell. They're wearing dark blue uniforms, armed to the teeth and equipped with the advanced technology that I saw them using a couple of weeks ago. I see that they are wearing the same reflective visors that Veronica Klaus's men were wearing in San Francisco.

Excellent.

There are probably twenty men in their small task force, and they make a beeline for the office. As they do, my men and I open fire on them. Our shots tear through the doors and the glass windows, razing the men down like pins at a bowling alley. The sound of gunfire is deafening. I take as many clean shots as I can, then spring from my position as several stragglers drag themselves away from the carnage.

"I'm covering you!" Uriah yells.

I move forward and roll into the hall, taking two more shots at the Omega stragglers. The first one goes down instantly, but my second shot hits the guard in the leg. He hits the ground and rolls onto his back, his finger squeezing the trigger of his automatic weapon. A spray of bullets cuts through the ceiling and nearly slices through my neck. I duck aside just in time – then Uriah is there, and he takes the kill shot, and the guard goes limp.

I look around me, breathing hard, wired. Twenty dead Omega troopers lie in the hall. Easy...almost too easy.

I grab a visor from one of the dead troopers and slip it over my head. I see a holographic image of the compound's layout, and radio chatter crackles through a microphone in the headset.

"Grab a visor!" I instruct. "Put it on and plug in!"

I touch the visor and swipe the screen to the left, and I stand there, amazed. A comprehensive map of every single thermal signature in the compound appears before me. There are a total of seventy-seven green tinted bodies – and thirty-five of them are red fighters, bodies not plugged into the Omega network – my men. Which leaves us with forty-four active hostiles in the building...and that's before backup shows up.

I can see that a group of men are working their way up the stairs from the second level, and that they are leaving behind ten special ops guys in the hallway in case we try to flee down the staircase.

"This is crazy!" Vera exclaims, slipping on the visor. "We can see it all!"

What makes the visor so unique is the fact that it does not obscure my vision in real-time. It only complements it. We assemble and crouch at the top of the staircase, waiting for the next round of troops to come up the stairwell. They hesitate for a moment, realizing that the sounds of gunfire have gone dead, and that nobody is responding to their radio call signs.

"Well, I wish I could speak French," Vera says.

"The radio isn't in French," I whisper. "It's Russian."

"Same thing."

Footsteps. Here comes a group of men moving up the stairwell, tight and fast, whisking forward in formation. There are only five of them, and I realize that they are probably the sacrifice. Too bad for them.

I take the first one, and Uriah, Vera and Andrew take the rest. We pick our way through their dead bodies, strewn across the stairs, their blood sprayed across the walls. We move to the second level. As the Omega visor indicated, there are bodies here, waiting. But we are ready, and I am anticipating them to take a shot at me from behind the left corner of the hallway.

We duck aside and arc to the right, shooting around the corner. I hear heavy grunting, followed by return fire. I pop a grenade from my belt and say, "GRENADE!" I pull the pin and fling it down the hallway and my men and I take cover behind the other side of the hall. The grenade detonates and shakes the walls, sending sharp bits of plaster and dust billowing through the hallway. I cough, covered in ghostly white paint particles, my ears ringing.

The white lights in the hallway flicker on and off, pulsing in rhythm with the red emergency lights in the ceiling. Somewhere, a siren begins to wail. There is no doubt about it – everybody in the entire base knows we're here now. There's no turning back.

"Keep moving, keep moving!" I yell.

We fight our way through every hallway in the second level, clearing out offices and flattening the Omega forces that barrel toward us, guns blazing. We adapt, improvise and overcome, just like Chris taught us to do so long ago.

It seems like hours, but we clear out the second level, and I radio Manny.

"Sundog, Second Level is cleared," I say. "Stand by."

"Roger that."

And then I radio the snipers. "Falcon Nest," I say, "this is Yankee Leader. You have a green light."

"Roger that Yankee Leader," one of them replies, a man with a gruff voice.

My snipers have been unleashed.

"One more level," I say, breathing hard, looking around the empty office. Computers are everywhere. What secrets do they contain?

"I'm with ya," Uriah replies, nodding.

We head to the first and final level. This is the worst level – the hardest. The thermal reader on the Omega visor is telling me that there are twelve men waiting for us here, and they are stationed in different corners of the room, waiting to ambush us from all sides as we come down the stairs. "Another grenade?" Uriah asks.

"Yeah," I reply. "Go for it."

Uriah tosses a grenade down the stairwell. We hang back and crouch low. It detonates and sends a choking wave of smoke up the stairs. We charge down to the final level, masked by the smoke and the confusion. Gunshots fly past me and ricochet off the metal railing on the stairwell. One of the Omega soldiers springs through the smoke and slams into me. I roll away and manage to get a shot at his head. He collapses, but a soldier follows closely behind him. He shoves my gun against my chest, knocking the wind from my lungs.

I hit the ground for the second time, scrambling backward. He grabs my ankle and drags me toward him. I twist around and kick him in the face with my free boot. I hear his nose crack as I break the cartilage. He doesn't break his hold, though. I struggle against him as he jams his knee into my chest, blood dripping from his face.

"Sie gehen zu sterben, Kommandant," he hisses. *You're going to die, Commander.*

"Not yet," I choke, grabbing the knife at my belt. I shove it upward and drive the blade into the soft flesh between his armor-plated vest and his belt. He screams and rears backward. I push him off me, pulling the knife out, staggering away. He holds the wound, seething, and lunges at me once more. But he is too slow. My rifle is already in my arms again, and I pull the trigger, my shot straight and true. He falls – dead.

I see Vera slip through the smoke and take a couple more shots, and then the rest of the Omega troopers on this level are dead. As the debris clears from the air, I can see that we are standing in the middle of a wide, open room, with a meeting table situated in the center. Maps and projectors are everywhere.

"Oh, my God!" Andrew exclaims. "This is an Omega strategy room. Incredible."

"Focus," I say. And then, "Sundog and Falcon Nest, Level One is cleared."

"Copy that, Yankee Leader," Falcon Nest replies. "We're taking heavy fire on the roof, but we're holding them off."

"Hang in there."

I cautiously approach the windows and peer outside. There is a large gravel driveway leading up to the compound, and beyond that, a concrete wall. Dead Omega soldiers are lying everywhere in the yard, shot by my snipers on the roof.

I can hear the rattle and boom of fire and return fire.

"The compound is ours," I say quietly.

"Yeah, baby!" Vera yells.

"We're not done yet," Uriah tells her, frowning. "Air support should be here in..." he checks his analog watch. "T-minus sixty seconds."

I close my eyes and pray.

So far it's going okay. So far, so far, so far...

We stay there, silently waiting, counting down the seconds until the Blackhawks will rumble overhead and bring punishment on the rest of the base. We wait and wait, and when the sixty seconds pass, I feel a tight knot of tension in my stomach.

"Where are they?" Vera asks.

Father Kareem approaches the window, slowly, his face tight.

"It could be..." he mutters, trailing off.

"*What?*" I ask.

Another sixty seconds. I radio the snipers on the roof. They see no sign of incoming air support. They're still taking heavy fire from Omega troopers on the outside of the walls.

"What is going on?" Vera yells, panic flashing in her expression. "Where is air support? They're a big part of this mission!"

"Mauve," Father Kareem says quietly.

"Excuse me?"

"President Mauve Bacardi," he goes on. "It is possible that she stood down on the Blackhawks."

"She doesn't have the authority to do that," I reply, jaw clenching. "Only Commander Davis would."

He gives me a long look.

"Commander Davis does take the advice of President Bacardi quite often, Commander Hart," he replies.

"You don't think she would keep the Blackhawks at Yukon, right?" I ask Uriah.

He exhales, tilting his head.

"I don't know, Commander. Mauve is very persuasive and Em Davis is very young."

Another sixty seconds. The Blackhawks are not here. They're either incredibly late or they never left at all.

"We're going to have to do this the hard way, aren't we?" Vera deadpans.

Andrew rests his arm on his knee.

"Yeah," he says. "It looks like it. Time for the backup plan."

"There really isn't a backup plan," I reply, "but okay."

"Enough talking," Uriah says. "Snipers are positioned on the roof, and they're taking heavy fire – but they're also giving it out. Everybody on the other side of that wall is focused on taking the compound back. I say we have the rest of Father Kareem's men and Elle and Cheng's detachment come in behind the Omega troops in front of the compound while we work our way out there. We can't get to them from inside the walls."

"What about the hostages upstairs?" I say. "Manny's platoon can't babysit them all day – we need those extra men."

"Tie them up, lock them in," Vera suggests. "They're office workers – barely soldiers. They're not the threat here."

I agree with her logic.

"Okay, and then what? We rush out the front gate? The Omega troopers outside on-base will take us out in seconds." I look at Uriah. "Unless the rest of our detachment with Elle and Cheng distracts them, like you said. That might take the pressure off us."

"Not to mention the snipers on the roof are doing a damn good job of keeping their forces from rushing us," Uriah adds.

Okay, so we have a plan. We can do this.

This base should be easy to take. We took down the whole building, didn't we?

We can tackle the next phase, no problem.

"Let's do it," I say. I check in through the radio, "Shadow One, this is Yankee Leader at the Compound. We want you to draw the enemy's fire in your direction."

"Copy that, Yankee Leader," Cheng's voice replies. "But what happened to our air support?"

"Don't know," I reply. "We're improvising."

"Roger that. We'll light them up for you, Yankee Leader."

"Good."

I look to Uriah.

"So we'll just hole up here until they can draw the outside fire in their direction," I say. "That will help our snipers on the roof, too."

Uriah glances at Father Kareem.

"What about the communication island?" he asks. "And the missiles – the Ship Killers?"

"The weapons will not be housed here," Father Kareem replies. "And the communication island is probably on lockdown. If Omega is proceeding according to their past procedures, they are most likely already evacuating the island and getting their people out."

"We have to stop them," I say.

The Blackhawks were originally supposed to circle the island and stop Omega from evacuating their workers there; we don't want to bomb or destroy the island. We want to preserve it. There is probably tons upon tons of valuable Omega intel that could help us win the war.

"Cassidy," Vera breathes.

"What?"

She nods toward the wall, eyes wide.

I follow her line of sight and feel a rush of recognition hit me:

There, on the wall, are pictures of Chris's face...and *my* face. I see my driver's license photo, and Chris's, too. I see sketches of me, black and white mug shots depicting my wild hair and freckles. There are other pictures, too: Vera Wright, Andrew Decker, even snapshots of Manny Costas and Elle Costas.

"What *is* all of this?" I breathe.

I walk to the wall, squinting through the hazy lighting at the rest of the wall. There are notes and papers tacked up, written in Russian and German. Some of it I understand. Some of it goes way over my head. On the far right of the room, there is a mug shot of Uriah. He looks younger, his hair shaved to the scalp in a tight, military-style haircut. He is glaring into the camera, and there is a number printed across the bottom of the photo.

I look at Uriah, startled.

"This is you," I say.

He stares at the photo, unflinching.

"Yeah," he replies.

"This is a mug shot."

"Yeah."

"You were *arrested*?"

He says nothing. There are a couple more pictures of Uriah, too; some sketches, some grainy snapshots.

"They were monitoring us," Andrew whispers. "All of us."

"Out of everybody in the militias...they were monitoring *us*?"

"We're the leaders. We're dangerous," Uriah says, simply.

I gasp, seeing a picture of Sophia Rodriguez in the right-hand corner. I want to cry, but I know better. It's just that I've never seen a picture of Sophia before...I met her after the Collapse, and the image of her face has always been preserved only in my memory. Seeing her in a photo like this...it's eerie.

"We'll come back for this stuff," I say. "We'll come back for all of it."

"Cassidy," Vera says. She points to another section of the wall. There is a map of Camp Freedom on it, along with names of militia leaders on the wall, mug shots arranged on a bulletin board, the pictures connected with red string. I see Commander Jones, Lieutenant Devin May, Lieutenant Vera Wright, and at the very top of the tree...my father.

Chapter Ten

Frank Hart. My father. His picture is an old snapshot from years ago – something that was stored away on a computer, in the digital cloud. He is wearing a gray T-shirt and a wide-brimmed sun hat. And the weird thing is that I'm sitting right next to him, maybe eight years old, my red hair long and wild, my hands covered in wet sand. We're at the beach, and what makes it more bizarre than anything else is the fact that nobody on this planet has seen this picture except for *me*.

How did Omega get this?

"My dad is dead," I say quietly. "Why are they still tracking him?"

"They're keeping tabs on all of the big militia leaders," Uriah replies, tense. "They may not know that he was killed in action in Sacramento."

I flinch when he says that. I don't like to talk about my dad like he's dead.

I like to talk about him like he's on some long vacation that he'll return from, when all of this crap is over. When the war is done and we've won and Omega is nothing more than a pile of rubble and ashes.

"How did they get this picture?" I say. "It was on a computer."

"I think it's fairly safe to assume that Omega can extract anything from anywhere," he replies.

"Yankee Leader," Cheng's voice crackles in my earpiece. "We're lighting them up. Make your move!"

I can hear the strain in his voice, and I know that we need to move.

"Let's roll out, guys," I say. "Stay tight and improvise."

We rush out the door to the compound, entering the gravel yard between the building and the concrete wall. The roar of gunfire is much louder out here. It pulls my head away from the puzzle of Omega's strategy room, their intense observation of my friends and I. I focus on the task at hand and everything else washes away.

We gather at the corner of the compound entrance. I nod at Uriah. He and ten of the men from the Angels of Death bust the gate open and storm outside in a solid wave, a sharp wall of bullets preceding them. I count under my breath and then yell, "Go, go, go!" And I bring the tail end of the platoon behind him with Father Kareem. We punch a hole through Uriah's line up like an arrowhead.

The base around us is fairly simple. Artificial streetlights illuminate a long road leading away from the compound and the visitor center. Every single Omega soldier on the base is out in full force, ebbing around the compound. A good chunk of them are engaged in a gunfight on the edge of camp – Cheng and Elle's detachment. Good. That leaves us a force of maybe seventy men out here.

The snipers on top of the roof of the compound have driven the Omega troops behind cover, so when we emerge, we're able to get to cover, too. I roll behind a parked Omega truck. Bullets pepper the side of the door as I crouch low, catching my breath.

"They are nearly in our grasp," Father Kareem says, breathing hard. "Lieutenant True can take the right, I'll take the left, and you take the center."

I look around us. In the dusky twilight, I feel like we're fighting in some in-between world, some purgatory of light and dark. Before us, there is a looped roadway that reconnects to the Glacier Spur Road, as the sign indicates. To the right, Omega troops are hiding behind two buildings, taking potshots across the asphalt. Uriah and his men are holding them off. To the left, more Omega troopers are staked out behind the temporary housing buildings. And directly in front of us, inside the loop, a smaller detachment of men are taking cover behind two vehicles.

"Okay," I say. "I'll cover you. Go."

Father Kareem shouts some orders at the Mad Monks in his wake and they break cover, heading to the left. I take some shots at the temporary buildings, giving Father Kareem time to reach a reasonable distance to start firing.

They clear the space, no problem.

"Okay," I say. I turn to Vera, who is waiting beside Andrew. "Center. Here we go."

"Yippi-kay-yay –" Andrew begins.

"Don't even finish that sentence," Vera deadpans. "Let's go."

So we do. We break, cover, too, and fire on the Omega troopers hiding behind the vehicles. They are vicious in their barrage of gunfire. I figure that I'm on a streak of using grenades today, so I pop one more and chuck it beneath the first truck they're hiding behind. The explosion bounces the vehicles and sends bits of hot metal and glass in all directions. My ears start ringing again, but I ignore it. We edge closer to the vehicles. The Omega troopers behind it are dead or dying. I see a bloody arm on the ground and a dead man lying beside it – his foot is also gone.

Beside him, there are two more dead Omega troopers. Dark, thick blood is pouring everywhere from their destroyed limbs. I look away, feeling sick, and keep moving. Because that is what good soldiers do – they keep going, even when the carnage is almost too much to handle.

The troopers beside them, behind the second vehicle, are scrambling for their weapons and their balance, stunned by the close proximity of the grenade detonation. I can see the sheer panic in their faces as we swoop around the corner, armed and ready to kill.

And we *do* kill them, swift Angels of Death, true to our name.

Every single one of the Omega soldiers in the center loop of the road is dead, and we are standing over their broken, dead bodies. I see Uriah moving in on the right, and Father Kareem sweeping the troops on the left. It occurs to me then, in a split second, that we are going to win this thing. That even without air support, we have still dominated our enemy. The element of surprise has been our greatest ally, and I feel a rush of grim pride.

We are the last fighters. We are fear itself.

"Cassidy, on your left!" Andrew yells.

I automatically duck right, and a bullet narrowly misses my skull. A lone Omega trooper, covered in blood, is taking wild shots from the end of the loop. He squeezes his trigger and holds tight, sending a tidal wave of gunfire through the air. Vera grabs my arm and shoves me aside, and the bullets miss both of us. We collapse on the ground in a tangled heap, her face sweaty and her hair hanging in greasy strands.

"Thanks," I say, quickly.

She rolls to her feet.

"Yeah, you got it," she replies.

I almost smile. Because somehow, despite our bickering and the shaky start Vera and I got off to so long ago, we have become strong allies in this fight against Omega.

The thunder of the fight rolls on, and as we clear out the base, we move toward Cheng and Elle's detachment, where they are bravely drawing Omega's fire. We come behind them in an arc, circling and striking quickly and efficiently.

Before long, they have fallen, too. I tap the visor and read the thermal signature map. I can see the signatures of my men, but there is a group of six bodies moving away from camp, up the trail, toward the Mendenhall Glacier.

Cheng breaks out of the foliage, breathless, his forehead streaked with blood, grasping Bravo's leash. The dog is wild-eyed and growling low, clearly agitated.

"They took *Elle*," he says.

"They took a hostage?" Vera gawks, unbelieving. "They're insane. We'll kill them."

My mind races. Elle – taken? I pull my balaclava off and wipe the thick layer of sweat that has accumulated on my face.

"We'll follow the thermal signatures," I say. "We can catch them before they get too far."

"I won't let them hurt her," Cheng tells me, his voice level.

"None of us will," I reply. "Vera? Stay with the men down here. Andrew, Cheng, you're with me." I look at Father Kareem. "Coming?"

A slight smile touches his face.

"I would delight in the challenge," he says.

"Sundog," I say into the radio. "Get your hostages wrapped up. The base is ours, but the communications island is still up for grabs."

I look across the water, toward the odd outcropping of land just beyond the compound, jutting into the icy lake. I can see the Omega aircraft lifting from the island, whisking their intelligence advisors and communications workers away.

I grit my teeth.

If we had air support right now, none of this would be happening. Every single person the communications island would be our prisoner right now.

Focus, Cassie. Get Elle. Then move on.

I feel a sharp spike of fear, afraid of losing Elle. That girl is special, and she's become a close friend. I can't stand the thought of something happening to her. I don't want to lose anybody else that I care about.

So Andrew, Cheng, and Father Kareem follow me into the trail. Bravo runs ahead of Cheng, occasionally stopping to pick up the scent trail. It's amazing, really – what we need advanced technology and thermal tracking to do, he can do with his nose.

We rush through the trail, every second taking Elle further and further away from us. I will not allow Omega to use her as a bargaining chip. If they've been monitoring us as closely as I think they have, then they will know that I will not allow Elle to die. Which makes her a valuable hostage – they can twist my arm if they have Elle.

They know it. I know it. And I'm going to stop them.

We run through the trees, popping out into a clearing. I can see the small detachment of escaping Omega soldiers in the distance – a blot of shadows moving across the rock. They scramble over a frozen waterfall, and then disappear into the icy depths of the towering glacier.

Their heat signatures vanish.

I take the visor off and toss it to the ground.

"Bravo can take it from here," I tell Cheng. "Let him work."

Cheng nods, understanding. The glacier is even bigger up close. It looms above our heads like a dark ice castle, full of cracks and crevices that would make even the most experienced climber cringe.

We move swiftly over rocks and gravelly terrain. Andrew slips once, but Father Kareem catches him. I tell myself that this will end well – that Elle will be unharmed, and that we will all return to Mendenhall Base victorious.

I skid to a halt at the side of the glacier. It is so massive – so incredible – that I can only stop and stare for a moment, amazed. It's unlike anything I've ever seen before, alien and beautiful all at once.

"We gotta go in there?" Andrew says, his voice sharp.

"Yeah," I reply.

Bravo tugs on his leash, desperate to keep moving, to keep tracking. His ears are flattened against his head, his fur stands on end. His dark eyes flash and I know that he is feeling the pressure of this battle just as much as we are.

By the time we actually reach the glacier itself, my legs are burning, muscles straining from pushing myself faster and faster, from climbing across rocks. When I look behind me, I see just how much distance we've covered – Mendenhall Base is a smudge in the distance.

Cheng says, "We have to go inside. There's no other way."

I look at the massive chunk of ice. Will it cave in on us? Will we be buried in the ice forever, our dead bodies preserved in the barren wilderness for centuries?

"Let's do this," I say. "But we're doing it the right way. Bravo leads – he clears the trail ahead of us, and then we follow. Keep your head down and open your eyes – they might be hiding right inside the cave, waiting to ambush us."

Cheng nods, and Andrew clicks a new magazine into his gun. Cheng gives Bravo the go-ahead and the dog slowly begins moving forward, sniffing the ground, moving across the gray and slick moonscape terrain, edging closer to the actual ice itself. He keeps moving, so we follow. I know that Bravo will be able to sense any weak spots or danger ahead – his senses are far more reliable than ours.

The ice is hard as a rock beneath my boots. Here, near the bottom, it is almost black, covered in a layer of dirt and gravel. We climb up the sloping glacier and reach the surface, where miles of frozen, blue waves stretch through the mountains.

Gorgeous. But I don't have time to admire the view. Maintaining my balance on the slick ice is difficult, and I stumble and fall several times. I wish that I had thought to bring some ice shoes or crampons; no such luck, though. We move forward, and then I slip again. But instead of just hitting the ground, the ice crumbles beneath my feet and I fall straight down. The air rushes out of my lungs as I realize that I have stepped into a hidden crevice in the ice. I twist and jam my leg against the glacier, wedging my back against the other edge. I stop falling, coming to a screeching halt, wedged between two walls of ice.

I look up, and I see Cheng, Andrew and Father Kareem peering down at me, maybe twenty feet above my head.

"Cassidy!" Andrew says. "Don't move, we'll pull you up!"

"With what?" I call back.

"Um, rope!"

My leg hurts. It pulses with aching pain, and I worry that I have broken it. I hope not – that would put a serious damper on my day. Several moments pass, and then Cheng and Andrew toss a rope to me. It lands just a few inches away. I lean forward and wrap the rope around my wrist, then sling it under my left arm. I brace myself against it.

"Ready?" I say.

"Ready," Cheng replies. "Hold on tight."

I grip the rope with all the strength that I have as they pull me up. I slowly move upward, and as I do, I dare a glance beneath me. Below, all I can see is black nothingness and the fresh scent of snow. I shudder and look up.

I was one second away from being buried alive.

When I reach the top, Father Kareem grabs my shoulders and pulls me onto the glacier again. I lay on my back, breathing hard, panting. My leg is throbbing. I sit up and look at it. I don't think it's broken; just sore and bloody from being used as an emergency brake.

"You okay?" Andrew asks, kneeling beside me.

"Yeah, just bruised," I reply. "This ice is dangerous."

"Yeah." He checks my leg. "You're scraped – maybe a little sprained. Can you walk?"

I take his hand and he pulls me to my feet. I test my weight on my leg. It hurts, but it's not unbearable. I've had worse. I'll be fine.

"I'm good," I say. "Let's keep moving."

So we do. We trek across the ice for what seems like an eternity before Bravo veers off course, a low growl rising in his throat. I follow his line of sight to the corner of the glacier, where a small piece of the ice juts into the mountains. At the very bottom of the seam, there is a small hole that tunnels inside the glacier.

The entrance to the ice caves.

Bravo approaches first. He clears it for us, and then we walk up to the cave, sharing concerned glances with each other. It's tiny – barely big enough for a full-sized person, let alone six Omega troopers and one hostage. They must have gone in single file.

"Cheng," I say. "You first."

He nods, and he ducks down under the ice with Bravo. I follow, with Andrew behind me and Father Kareem bringing up the rear. I flick the flashlight of my rifle on as the tunnel of ice closes in around us. Complex walls of clear blue ice encapsulate us as we move. I tell myself not to be claustrophobic, but it's a little difficult to forget that we are tunneling beneath tons of melting, shifting ice.

Sounds fun, right? I think. *Chris would be loving this.*

The ice around us is freezing cold, but the air coming from within the caves smells oddly stale – like it's been circulating for thousands of years. And hey, it probably has.

We move quickly but cautiously, listening for the sounds of the Omega soldiers ahead of us, leery of every corner. We don't speak if we can help it, controlling our breathing. In several places, the cave gets smaller and smaller. We have to get down on all fours to squeeze through.

At last, we come to a large, open area in the cave. I stand upright, thankful for the headspace. Bravo growls again. He pulls Cheng toward the corner of the ice room. A tunnel curves away from here, into the very heart of the glacier, wide and tall.

"Set up a marker," I tell Andrew. "We don't want to get lost in here."

Andrew nods and kneels to the ground, stacking a cairn with the loose rocks in the cave. I beam my flashlight back toward Bravo. His eyes glow in the light, and he looks like he's ready to take a bite out of somebody's arm.

We keep going, moving down the large tunnel to the left, picking our way through rocks and loose gravel. Every so often, Andrew stops and stacks another cairn, making sure to mark our progress through this twisting, disorienting world of frozen water.

Bam!

A gunshot echoes through the cavern, and a bullet wedges itself into the ice right beside Cheng's head. He immediately hits the ground, as we all do. I flick my flashlight off. Ahead of us, there is another opening into an air pocket in the ice. I see the briefest flicker of shadowy movement up ahead, and then there is suffocating silence again.

My heart races, my hands sweat.

It's us against them in this darkness. We have to be smart. In this kind of terrain, there's no good way to tell where we're actually shooting – and whether or not we're accidentally shooting at Elle.

And then a voice cuts through the silence: "RUN, GO BACK!"

It's Elle's voice. I immediately gauge the distance between me and her voice, and I decide to take the chance. I surge forward, following the wall, and skid into the empty room. I see shadows at the far end, and just as I'm raising my rifle into my shoulder, Bravo streaks past me, a bullet in the darkness. His growl is vicious, and unlike me, he is not handicapped by the lack of lighting here.

I am about to take a shot at one of the shadows in the darkness when a thundering, piercing detonation rocks the entire cave. It throws me forward. I land on my chest, face scraping against the rock. Pieces of ice and rock fall all around me, and I hear a loud rushing, cracking noise. Panic grips me – is the glacier collapsing on us? What exploded?

I scramble to my hands and knees, head spinning, and try to get a grip. I flick on the flashlight of my rifle and beam it backward. Behind me, there is a solid wall of freshly crumbled ice, cutting me off completely from Cheng, Father Kareem and Andrew.

No, no, no, no.

I hear a snap, a crack. Red, hellish light illuminates the cavern, and I see them: all six of them, Omega soldiers with their visors pulled back. The red light is coming from flares that they have thrown on the ground. Someone screams bloody murder, and I see Bravo latched onto the arm of the trooper on the far right, standing guard over Elle.

The girl's hands are tied in front of her, and she is bleeding from her forehead. She is screaming commands at Bravo. A trooper raises his gun and aims at me, shock flashing across his face. I don't think that I am supposed to be on this side of the collapsed ice. I roll aside, missing his shot. I raise my rifle into my shoulder and squeeze the trigger, hitting him in the shoulder. He stumbles backward, and as he is falling to the ground, I shoot him once more – permanent.

That takes out one. Five more to go.

I kneel and take aim at the trooper who is heading toward Bravo with a knife. I shoot him, and he falls dead.

Four more.

Elle suddenly springs upward and lands a perfect, powerful roundhouse kick to the face of one of the troopers. She hits the ground on her side, teeth gritted, and then Bravo jumps up and takes a slicing bite out of his shoulder, between his neck and the body armor. He screams and tries to scramble away, but Bravo's grip is as strong as iron. I sling the rifle over my shoulder and pull the knife from my belt.

I am afraid to do any more shooting in this room – I don't want to get buried down here under tons of ice. I sprint forward and come up behind the trooper who is currently being used at Bravo's chew toy. I slip the blade of my knife between his ribs. He gasps, and then slowly goes still, blood bubbling from his mouth.

"Out, out, Bravo!" Elle yells.

Bravo releases the dead man, blood dripping from his jowls. He is *scary*.

Only two more. I turn around, and I see that the two remaining Omega troopers are fleeing. One of them lays down a long burst of cover fire as his comrade turns tail, heading toward a tiny crevice twisting away from this ice room.

I quickly cut the ties on Elle's wrists and hand her my knife. She flashes a dangerous smile and springs forward. "GET HIM, BRAVO!" she shouts.

And just like that, the dog is gone, springing toward the first trooper. Bravo runs, jumps, and clamps his sharp teeth onto his arm. The Omega trooper stumbles, yelling, using the butt of his rifle to try and beat Bravo off his arm. But Elle is there, and she makes quick work of him with the knife. With a single swipe of her arm, she cuts his throat open, and he hits the ground, dead.

Just one more left.

I look at Elle.

"Take care of the last one," I say.

She nods, and she and Bravo vanish into the small tunnel. I catch my breath then kneel down, talking into my radio. "Shadow One, this is Yankee Leader. Do you read me?" I ask.

Static.

Then, "Yankee Leader, this is Blade Two, I read you. Where are you?"

Uriah.

"We're in the glacier," I reply. "I'm cut off from the rest of team, there was an explosion. The ice caved in, and we're sealed off."

"You're stuck in the glacier?" he replies.

"Yeah."

More static. Then I hear Andrew's voice, "Yankee Leader, what's your status? Are you guys okay?"

"Troopers are down, package has been retrieved," I reply. "But we're stuck here."

"Are there any other exit points from the space you're in?"

"There's a tunnel that winds north."

"Take it. Find a hole and get to the surface."

"Roger that."

"Yankee Leader, this is Blade Two again," Uriah replies. "Don't take any chances. The glacier is dangerous. Find an exit point and we'll meet you there."

"What's the status of the base?" I ask instead, moving forward, ignoring his advice.

"We've taken it," Uriah replies. "But everybody on the comm island has pretty much made a clean exit."

I exhale. At least we still have the hostages in the compound with Manny's platoon.

I cut down the tunnel, where Elle is crouched over the dead body of the last Omega trooper. She glances at me just as Bravo does, their eyes both flashing in the beam of my flashlight. In that moment, I'm almost afraid of her, but then I shake myself and say, "Good work."

She slowly stands up, wipes the blood from her cheek and says, "Thanks for coming after me.""We don't leave anybody behind," I reply, simply. "And neither does your dog."

Elle smiles.

"Bravo is the best friend I've ever had," she tells me.

"Well, hopefully I am, too." I raise my eyebrows. "Ready to get out of here?"

"Totally ready."

We move forward, through the endless curves and twists of the ice cavern. My platoon checks in with me via the radio. They are going back up to the surface to see if they can find a way to get to us.

"They just grabbed me at the last second," Elle says. "I was fighting, and I think they got desperate. They knew the base was falling, so they took off and abandoned the rest of their troops fighting our militia. Cowards." She spits on the ground. "There was just too many of them, and I got separated from Cheng and the rest of the platoon during the firefight."

"I'm glad you're okay," I say.

"Me too." She looks up. "This place is kind of eerie."

"Beautiful, but eerie, yes."

"Wow, look." She points up ahead. We come to another ice chamber, but the inside of this one is filled with a frozen pool of water. Droplets of water are dripping from the ceiling in staccato rhythm, like rainfall.

"It's melting?" Elle says, puzzled. "It's the dead of winter."

"It's warmer down here than it is up there," I point out. "Also, yeah, it probably melts a little bit every year."

"How long do you think this glacier has been here?" She looks at me, and I see a spark of childlike curiosity in her eyes. It's the first time I've seen a flash of that in Elle – usually she is so contained, so wise beyond her years.

"Probably centuries," I shrug. "I mean, this was water before it froze."

"Maybe it was the flood."

"Maybe."

"Maybe it was an ice age."

"Could have been."

She holds her hand out and the water touches her skin. She takes handfuls of it and washes the blood off her face. "I like it down here," she says. "Too bad we can't stay."

"Living in a glacier doesn't really appeal to me," I say. "Come on."

We keep moving, tunneling through every free space beneath the glacier. Several times, we run into a dead end or a passageway too narrow to squeeze through, which forces us to reroute and try a different tunnel.

I stop and turn around, seeing ice all around me. I close my eyes, forcing myself to take a deep breath. "We're lost," I say.

"We're not lost," Elle replies. "We're just *turned around*. It's impossible to know where these passageways go. There's got to be another opening somewhere."

"There better be."

I chew on my lower lip, irritated. Every second I stay under this glacier is another second that I can't be out on the base, overseeing the progression of our takeover. I know that Uriah, Vera and Manny can handle it, but still. I need to be back, as soon as possible.

"Commander," Elle says as we walk, ducking under another ice ceiling. "I want you to know that I'm sorry about what happened in Yukon City. At the Mess Hall." She lowers her voice. "I shouldn't have lost my temper like that. I started the fight – I caused the whole problem with President Bacardi."

"You were acting on instinct," I say. "I can't fault you for that."

"But I knew better."

"Elle," I reply. "You're a fighter, just like me. Sometimes, people push us too far and things happen. It's not your fault – it's in the past, now. Don't worry about it."

She goes silent for a little while, then says, "I'm glad I joined the militias. Before, it was just me and

Bravo, surviving. Now we have a purpose, a reason to keep going."

"I know the feeling," I admit.

"There's something about being with you guys. The comradery, I guess."

"It keeps us alive. It gives us hope."

"If we lose this war, I'll still be glad that I stood up and fought."

I smile sadly.

"Me too," I say. "We are the last fighters."

She whispers, "We are fear itself."

And then the moment is broken, because Bravo barks softly and begins trotting down the tunnel.

I've found something! he seems to say.

Elle perks up and jogs behind him. I follow, and then I see why Bravo is so excited. I smell the rush of cold air from the outside world, and I see a small crevice in the glacier, leading up to the top of the ice.

"Score," Elle says. "We're out."

Chapter Eleven

When we come back to the surface, I take a breath of cold, pure air. I climb carefully to the top of the glacier, Bravo and Elle clambering up behind me. We leave the alien, frozen world of ice behind us and I peer into the distance. Across the lake, I see the communications island writhing in orange flames. The radio waves are jumbled with frenzied dialogue and call signs.

"Shadow One," I say. "Shadow One, this is Yankee Leader. Come in."

Nothing.

Elle and I share a worried glance, then head across the glacier as quickly as we can, watching for crevices and potholes. It takes us half an hour to make it to the sheer rocks propped up against the ice wall. I can see that Andrew, Cheng and Father Kareem are at the bottom, looking worn and weary.

"You made it," Andrew says. "Good."

I don't reply. I'm too busy concentrating on getting good handholds on the rock face as I climb down. My boots slip against the slick granite and slushy moss a few times, but I manage to make it all the way to the bottom without breaking my neck.

"What happened in there?" Andrew asks as my feet hit the dirt.

"I think they detonated a grenade," I say. "They caused a cave-in."

"That was stupid," Andrew replies. "They could have caused a massive shift inside the glacier and killed all of us."

"Nobody ever accused the Omega grunts of being smart."

"True that."

Elle and Bravo arrive next. Cheng wraps Elle into a tight, desperate embrace. She hugs him back and I see the traces of a smile on her lips.

"Worried about me, eh?" she asks.

"I was worried about the dog, obviously," Cheng replies, taking a step back. He pats Bravo on the head. "I'm glad you're okay."

Elle rolls her eyes.

"Commander, something is wrong on base," Father Kareem. "We must return at once."

"Working on it," I reply.

We sweep forward, limping, bloody, tired. I try making radio contact with my men on the base, but nobody is answering their call signs. Something dark and fearful settles in my stomach. We move faster, fear and dread giving us the adrenaline rush we need to make it back to the base.

At last, after an eternity of walking and fighting our way through trails and shrubbery, we arrive onsite again. Cars are turned upside down, and the dead bodies of dozens of Omega troopers lay in the streets. There is so much blood – it literally pools on the asphalt and runs into the gutters, staining the snow.

The power of my militia and the Mad Monks almost frightens me.

Almost.

The compound is locked down by the Angels of Death. My earpiece is still nothing but loud, screeching static, so I remove it from my ear and let it hang on my vest. At the lookout point near the compound, I spot Uriah standing with his boot on the railing. I approach, slowly, and say, "Uriah."

He turns quickly, surprised. And then he springs forward and embraces me, smelling like blood and smoke. "You're okay," he breathes. "Thank God."

I squeeze him and pull back, looking at his face.

"Yeah," I say. "We made it. We got Elle."

"Good."

"What's going on here? The radios aren't working."

Uriah grimaces.

"Nobody's radio is working," he replies. "They self-destructed the communications island, and they detonated some kind of frequency disrupter. Our radios are down."

I mutter a curse under my breath.

"And the hostages?" I ask.

"Tied and packaged up with a nice little bow."

"Casualties?"

Here, he smiles. "This time, we have none on our side."

I exhale.

"Wow," I say. "We did good."

"But we lost the island."

"That's not so good. What about the Ship Killers – the rockets?"

"We're assuming they're in the armory."

"Crap, I really didn't want to lose the island."

I feel a pang of bitter disappointment. Whatever was on that island was important enough to Omega for them to destroy the entire building before we got our hands on it. What secrets did it hold? Could it have changed the course of the war for us?

Don't think about that now. You've taken the base. Good job!

I look to Father Kareem.

"I want you and your men to do a full sweep of this area," I say. "Check for any Omega stragglers or survivors. If you find anyone, bring them back for questioning. If they fire on you, kill them."

"As you wish, Commander Hart," Father Kareem says, bowing slightly.

He retreats with several members of the Mad Monks to carry out my orders.

"Elle," I say. "Find a medic and get cleaned up. Uriah, come with me."

Elle and Cheng head across the road with Bravo, toward the medivac teams who are picking their way through the base, looking for wounded militiamen who may need assistance.

"You need medical attention, too," Uriah points out as we walk toward the compound. "What happened to your leg?"

"I fell down a hole."

He smirks. "That sounds like something you'd do."

"Ha. Ha."

We reach the compound, and Vera is standing outside, reloading her gun. She looks up at me, irritation flickering across her face.

"Where's Andrew?" she asks, simply.

I jerk my thumb over my shoulder, indicating that he is still staring at the communications island, festering in flames.

"Did you get Elle?" she says.

"Yeah," I answer.

"Good." She slings her gun over her shoulder. "The hostages upstairs are going crazy."

"Define crazy."

"A few of them started putting curses on us," she goes on. "Witchcraft and all that crap."

I make a face.

"That's weird."

"You should go see for yourself."

"Thanks, I will."

I go back inside the compound, into the first level. The strategy room has been cleared of the thick, acrid smoke. I step over the dead bodies of fallen Omega troopers as I study the boards again, filled with pictures of me, Chris and dozens of other militia leaders. I raise a hand to my mouth.

"Uriah," I say, "look!"

He follows my line of sight and his eyebrows go up.

"Wow," he mutters.

It's not just us Omega has been monitoring. Each wall has the main militia leaders from every state in the country, from California to Boston, Massachusetts. I breathlessly filter through the names and the face – young, old, male, female. I see pictures of different militia uniforms and names: *The Rattlers* in Texas, *The Killers* in Arizona, *The Bloodhounds* in Georgia, *The*

Gators in Florida, *The Brigadiers* in Pennsylvania. Hot tears form in my eyes.

For the first time since we started fighting in the mountains – since Omega came and we took a stand – I know, without a doubt, that we are not alone. There are other militias, all across the country. There are so many listed on the walls that I lose count.

And not only that, but many of the militia locations correspond with the information logged away in my head concerning the nuclear weapons that Arlene told me about.

These militias are not just rebelling – they're *armed.*

"People are fighting back," I say, looking at Uriah. "They're *fighting back.*"

He nods, slowly, as shocked as I am.

This could change everything. Imagine if all of us were to unite? A massive, united force against the biggest global invasion army of all time. It would be the battle of the century – perhaps the gateway to World War Three…if we're not already in the midst of it.

I place my hand on the wall, leaning over my father's picture at the top of the board. I remove it from the wall and hold it in my hands, studying the wrinkles around his eyes and the careless smile on his face.

I miss you, Daddy.

I fold the picture and slip it into my pocket. Uriah and I move upstairs, overwhelmed with this new knowledge – the knowledge that the West Coast is not alone in fighting Omega – and that we never were.

Chris, I wish you were here! You should know this – it would change everything!

We reach the third level, where Manny is in the hallway with some men. He is bathed in sweat but his eyes sparkle with energy.

"Cassidy, my girl," he says. "Come to gawk at the Omegans in their natural habitat?"

I look behind the glass window, into the office. The hostages are lined in a neat row, their wrists tied together. Militiamen are guarding them. Some of the hostages look terrified. They are shaking and pale. One of them has vomited in the corner, and another's forehead is bathed in blood from a head wound.

"Do they speak English?" I ask.

"Most of them do," Manny replies. "A few only speak Chinese or Arabic. There's a few Russian natives in there, too. But they're all fairly bilingual – I guess they have to be to keep up with our militia intel."

Makes sense. One of the hostages – a tall, Asian man with short black hair – is glaring at me. His gaze is steely and unwavering, and his eyes never move from my face.

"Who's that guy?" I ask.

"The happy-go-lucky one?" Manny replies. "He's the Intelligence Supervisor, according to what we found. Basically, he's the head honcho of level three. They're superstitious suckers, too, let me tell ya. They're promising that we're all going to die and that the devil will bring our 'just-desserts,' as he says."

And based on the super-sized hate glare he's sending my way, he means it.

"I want him interrogated," I say. "I want to know everything he knows. Codes and passwords on every computer, disabling alarm systems, shutting down communication systems and barring the Omega satellites from connecting with this compound."

"And if he doesn't comply?" Manny asks, raising an eyebrow.

I think about all of the horrible things Omega has done to us.

"He will," I say. "Eventually."

Manny nods, understanding.

Uriah says, "You should just kill him. He's not going to tell you anything."

I glance at Uriah. He is staring at the Intelligence Supervisor, concerned.

"He might," I reply.

"No. Not this guy. He's a killer – that's it."

"He's a computer guy, not an assassin."

"I just know," Uriah insists. "He's not going to talk."

I shake my head.

"Carry on, Manny," I say.

"You got it, Commander."

"We need to set up some kind of communication with Sector 27," I tell Uriah, as soon as Manny moves down the hall. "Chris needs to know about the other militias. Think of the reinforcements! It would be a game-changer if every militia from all of the fifty states united as one. Plus, he needs to know that we've seized all of the weapons here."

"It could be trouble," Uriah replies. "All of those militias, with all of those commanders. Who's going to be in charge of all of them?"

"It's an alliance, Uriah. They answer to their own commanders."

"It could complicate things."

"It could *end* all of this. Things could go back to the way they were!"

Of course, things will never be exactly like they were before the Collapse. I doubt McDonald's will ever make a reappearance in the post-apocalyptic landscape of North America. But hey – a girl can dream, right?

"It's never going to end," Uriah replies, darkly. "This doesn't stop. Ever."

When I look at Uriah in this moment, I realize something that I have never realized before: he does not want this war to end. In this war, Uriah has found his true identity. In that way, we are the same. But I want this battle to come to a positive conclusion.

Not Uriah. I can see it in his eyes, the bloodlust, the thirst for the adrenaline rush of a tactical mission, the sheer excitement of hand-to-hand combat. This is Uriah. This is *who he is.*

This revelation startles me, and I take a step backward.

"It will end," I say. "Regardless of *how* it ends, it *will.*"

Uriah says nothing.

"Uriah, you have to accept that," I tell him.

"I'll accept it when you do," he replies, flicking his dark gaze to mine.

I look away.

"Whatever," I mutter.

Uriah takes a step forward, pressing his lips against my ear.

"You love it as much as I do," he whispers. "We're both creatures of war."

I jerk back, inhaling.

"You're wrong," I say. "I'm not."

He just smiles.

And as he does, a cold chill runs up my spine.

***

Twilight comes sometime during mid-morning. I'm standing on the roof of the compound with my arms folded across my chest, watching the dim, pinkish glow of half-light illuminate the surface of the Mendenhall Glacier. I take a deep breath and imagine, just for a moment, that I am somewhere peaceful and safe, and then I open my eyes and accept the events of the day.

Andrew and the tech team downstairs have been working feverishly to restore radio communications with Yukon City. By extension, they are trying to open up radio waves with California and Sector 27, so that we can tell Chris that there are militias everywhere. California is not alone – there are people who might be able to help us. More reinforcements than merely the Mad Monks.

This revelation could change the course of the war. With one, small piece of intelligence like this, we could become more powerful than ever before. We may be able to push Omega's foot army out.

In the distance, I hear the steady, lone sound of a helicopter. I recognize it instantly, and I turn around, climbing the stairs to the top level, working my way to the third one where Manny is, and then finding Uriah.

"There's aircraft coming in," I say.

"Enemy?" he replies, straightening.

"Don't know."

I tell Manny to come with me, leaving the hostages with Vera's platoon. We reach the first level of the compound. By the time we get there, everyone has gathered outside. The small beat of helicopter blades has become a physical thing – a gray Apache chopper is coming from the northwest.

"It's one of ours," Father Kareem states, simply, studying the aircraft with an expression of mild interest on his face. "I do not believe that we are in danger."

I take his word for it – I have to.

The chopper slowly gets closer, then lowers itself to the ground on the photo point overlooking the lake. The din of its blades fills the camp, whipping loose dirt and rocks everywhere. I approach it, shielding my eyes with hands, Manny and Uriah with me.

The blades slowly wind down and the door opens. A woman jumps out, hauling a rifle and a backpack. She straightens up and heads straight toward me.

"Commander Davis?" I say, frowning. "What are you doing here?"

She grimaces, but continues to move toward me, stopping when she is just a few feet away from my position.

"Commander Hart," she says. "We need to talk."

I glare at her, remembering how, just a few hours ago, we were denied air support from Yukon City. How her leadership, influenced by Mauve Bacardi, could have gotten my men killed.

"Yeah," I reply. "We do."

She nods, then looks at Uriah. His eyes are stone cold. She averts his gaze and nods toward the compound. "Can we go in there?" she asks.

I nod, and she begins walking toward the building – her steps are hurried and her eyes are bloodshot. I wonder why she is here, and what's wrong.

"You sense something fishy here?" Manny whispers.

"Yeah," I answer. "Let's find out what it is."

We head back to the compound, into the first level. The bodies of the dead Omega troopers have been cleared out, leaving only bloodstains on the floors and walls. The intelligence boards are still up, displaying militia information and photos for Em to see as she walks in. Her eyes widen, and then she returns her gaze to me.

"This is incredible," she says, breathless. "This... Is it true?"

"It's true," I reply. "Omega's been monitoring the militias from this base."

"Dear God. I thought we were alone." She places her hand on her chest, as if to calm herself. "Commander, I'm sorry about the air support. I did not plan on revoking it."

"You're going to be more than sorry," Uriah mutters.

I hold my hand up, and he falls silent.

"I'd like an explanation," I tell her.

"We were attacked," she says.

I stare at her.

"*What?*"

"We were attacked by our own people."

"Are you serious?"

"The civilians staged a coup." She shrugs. "They were trying to assassinate Mauve Bacardi. It was...*bloody*. We weren't prepared for it. We've always been prepared for a lot of things, but an attack from the civilians was not one of them."

"Is President Bacardi still alive?" I ask.

"Yes. She's in ICU; she might survive, she might not." Em leans against the wall, and in that moment I see how tired she is. Like me, she is worn out by the aggressive society this apocalypse has created. "The point is," Em goes on, "we were under attack, and we couldn't get the choppers off the ground in time. It was my fault, and I'm sorry."

I lick my lips. I take a deep breath. And then I say, "Don't let it happen again."

She nods.

"What's the state of Yukon City now?" I ask.

"We've got the civilians under control," she replies. "But there was a high casualty count. Over one hundred and fifty dead refugees."

"God, that's horrible," I say. "How did they attack?"

"They stormed the Begich Towers," Em answers. "They were trying to reach Mauve's office. They got past the guards – killed three of them – and dragged her into the streets. They did horrible things to her, Commander. And all this time I thought she was invincible – incapable of unpopularity."

"What did Mauve do to them?" I ask. "Something made them turn on her."

"She started taking their food rations and giving it to the National Guard and the militias," Em tells me. "It wasn't out of hate or selfishness. It was just fear. She was afraid we'd starve."

"I thought you guys had farms and livestock."

"Most of it is depleted," she admits. We have a lot, but not enough to support a population as big as Yukon City. We were never meant to expand this much."

"So the people are starving, and they rebelled, and they needed somebody to crucify," I say. "Mauve Bacardi was the number one target."

"Exactly."

"I guess that leaves you in charge of Yukon City, Commander Davis," I say. "So you should get out of here and go back."

I know I sound cold and uncaring, but facts are facts.

"I had to make contact with you somehow," she says, as if not hearing me. "I couldn't get you guys on the radio, and I had to find out if you had taken the base or not."

"Omega sent out a frequency disruptor," I reply. "Our radios are down."

"I can't believe you took this base. This was the impossible feat. You and your men...you're dangerous. No wonder Omega hates you."

I feel a bit of pride swell up within me when she says that.

"You're not just here to apologize," I state, making an educated guess. "There's something else that you came here to tell me."

Em's eyes drop to the ground.

"Is it that obvious?" she asks.

I say nothing. My silence speaks for itself.

"Yeah," she says at last. "That's not the only reason."

"Spill."

She drops her backpack on one of the strategy tables, a look of pain flickering across her features. "There's something that Mauve kept from you," she says. "I mean, there's something we *both* kept from you."

I frown.

"Okay, what is it?"

"We have nuclear subs in the harbor at Whittier, in Yukon City," she says. "It's our big secret, and it's the real reason the militias were assigned to the middle of Alaska.

We're here to protect the subs. Arlene Costas never lied to you about the weapons in Yukon City. They're there. All of them."

I fold my arms. I remember seeing the black subs sitting in the harbor, thinking that they were simply old relics from a war fought decades ago; the Cold War, World War Two. All this time...right in front of us?

"You have *nuclear* subs?" I say.

"Yes," she replies. "Five of them, ballistic submarines. Each is capable of launching ballistic missiles on multiple targets, and they all carry at least one nuclear warhead."

"Whoa, hold the phone," Manny exclaims. "You're telling us, that all this time, while we've been screwing around trying to find recruits and infiltrating Omega bases and the West Coast is being bombed to kingdom come, you all have been sitting on nuclear subs with ballistic capabilities and you didn't *tell us?*"

His face is flushed red. He is angry.

"It was a militia secret," Em says. "If the information were to fall in the wrong hands, Omega would have used it. You know that. You've seen how they worm their way into every level of society –every branch of leadership. I wanted to tell you, but I couldn't. I didn't trust you with the weapons."

I place my hand on Manny's arm, attempting to calm him.

"You didn't trust us?" I echo. "The fate of the free world is at stake. I would suggest you get over your trust issues."

I'm sorry." She looks like she's going to cry. "I didn't want anybody else to die...but now, I can see that no matter what, people *are* going to die." She heaves a great sigh. "I know that turning the weapons over to you now will be the best thing for us in the long run."

"Where did these subs come from?" I ask.

"They're Cold War subs," she goes on. "The civilians are totally in the dark about their capabilities. Mauve, myself and Colonel Wilcox of the National Guard are the only ones who are aware of the ballistic subs' load."

Manny's eyes flicker.

"Did Arlene know?" he asks, his voice low.

Em looks at him.

"She knew that we had weapons," she tells him. "But that's all. I swear."

Manny doesn't reply, but he looks a bit deflated.

"So did the slaughter of the civilians suddenly trigger your forthrightness or what?" Uriah asks, cold. "In my book, you screw us over once, and the trust is gone."

"Like I said, the time has come to let someone know," Em replies. "And if it's going to be anyone, it should be you, Commander Hart. And Commander Chris Young. Your militias are doing something right – something selfless, something heroic. I know that you'll use the subs for the greater good. I was wrong to misjudge you, and so was Mauve."

I pull a chair out from beneath one of the strategy tables and plop down on it, taking this information in. Another bombshell on another red-letter day for Cassidy Hart.

"So we've got nuclear warheads sitting in the harbor at Yukon City," I say.

"And biochemical weapons," Em adds. "You can attach the biochemical weapon to the ballistic missiles and strike any city along the coastline without poisoning the entire state with radiation fallout."

"What kind of biochemical weapons are you talking about?" I ask.

"Sarin gas, the same stuff Omega has used against us. It's odorless and tasteless. It touches your skins and kills you, and it leaves no residue behind."

"Just the dead bodies," I whisper.

"Commander, just think about what we could do with this weaponry."

"The United States doesn't fight with biochemical weapons."

"We do now," Uriah interjects. "Whatever treaty or agreement the United States was held to

241

disintegrated when the country collapsed. Sarin gas isn't off the table for us. Not now."

"We can kill Omega without killing the earth," Manny says, staring at the wall. "Cassidy, are you hearing this?"

I nod, vaguely.

"This is the opportunity we've been waiting for," Uriah goes on. "We've got *nuclear weapons.* We've got bioterrorism capabilities. This is our *moment.*"

"Uriah," I say. "Keep it down."

I look around, suddenly paranoid that someone else has overheard our conversation. If this intel gets out to the wrong people, the information could leak to Omega, and they would anticipate our next move.

"This is a whole new level of warfare," I say quickly. "We gotta be careful."

"Careful?" Uriah slams his fist on the table. "Dammit, Cassidy. Omega has taken EVERYTHING from us. To hell with *careful!*"

I don't flinch.

"What about the civilians or survivors who might be hiding along the coastline?" I ask. "If we send these weapons out to strike Omega, we could be killing our own, too."

"That's a sacrifice we'll have to make," Uriah says.

"We're trying to preserve what we have left, not destroy it."

"There's no other way."

"There has to be!" I yell. Hot tears form in my eyes. "I don't want to do this, Uriah. I don't want to be the one responsible for pulling the trigger on the West Coast."

"No," Uriah replies, grim. "But you'll be responsible for letting California fall to Omega, which is the same thing. So I ask you this: would you rather be the one, or would you rather *they* do it?"

"That's not a fair argument," I mutter.

"You know I'm right. We came here for *weapons*! We came here for an advantage – well, this is it! You have to be willing to hit the red button, Cassidy."

I say nothing. To do this would be to unleash instant death upon the Omega hotspots along the coast – San Francisco, Monterey, and Los Angeles. Places where Omega has congregated in the thousands.

"And what advantage would this give us, really?" I say. "Other than killing their men? Because we know there's more men where they came from."

"Omega would fear us," Em replies quietly. "They would know that we could retaliate with something far more dangerous than a simple tactical strike mission or seizing their bases. And they would not just see the threat of such a biochemical weapon, but the results of it. It would shock them – it would show them that we mean business."

I consider this. I know she's right...but I cannot get Chris's voice out of my head.

Think about what you're shooting at before you pull the trigger. You can't take back a bullet, Cassie. You gotta be sure.

"Em," I say, shaky. "Are you willing to take a step away from President Bacardi and Yukon City? Can you help us?"

Em raises an eyebrow, and then, ever so slowly, a small smile touches her lips.

"What are you asking me to do?" she says.

"Pull the National Guard out of Whittier and station them here, in the occupied Mendenhall Base," I tell her. "We've got hostages here, and seized weapons and intel. We can't afford to lose this stronghold."

"And?" Em said.

"You and your militia come with me back to California," I continue. "You reinforce the Freedom Fighters, and you help us keep Omega off the coastline."

"I only have three hundred men in my militia," she says.

"Three hundred is great."

245

"Three hundred plus your force…that's not enough to stop Omega."

"It is if we utilize the nuclear subs and the ballistic weaponry." I look at Uriah. "Right?"

He dips his head, solemn.

"After we kick Omega out of California with the subs' weapons," I go on, swallowing, "we unite the militias around the country and form a strong front against any more attacks."

"What if Omega just nukes us all and washes their hands of us?" Manny points out.

"They won't. They want to use this country, not destroy it." I level my gaze. "We have to show them that we mean business – that we will fight fire with fire if we have to. If Omega wanted California wiped off the map, they would have done it a long time ago."

If Uriah is right in his line of thinking, they'll probably back off.

And if they back off, that will be the first small victory that will lead to big ones.

"So what are we doing, then?" Uriah asks.

"We're going back to Yukon City," I reply. "We're taking the subs down the coastline, and we're launching the ballistic weapons at San Francisco, Monterey and Los Angeles, and every Omega stronghold in between."

"We can join up with the California militias in San Diego," Em interjects, her voice trembling with excitement. "It's a stronghold, now. We can depend on them."

"So you're in?" I ask.

She nods. "I'm all in."

I tap the holster on my belt.

"Let's do this," I say.

Chapter Twelve

I sleep lightly on the top level of the compound, in an empty office. The order has gone out to my troops that we will be returning to Yukon City, but the exact circumstances have remained secret. I cannot have the information about the ballistic submarines getting out. Uriah and I know; Em knows, Vera, Manny, Cheng and Elle know. But that is it.

I wake up, slowly, at about 0500, groggy and sore. I stretch my leg out, squeezing it, checking for any unusual pain. It's bruised and scraped from my fall through the ice, but nothing too major. For that, I am grateful. It could have been so much worse.

Are we really going to unleash these weapons? I think.

Yeah, I guess we are. Omega has finally driven us to this point.

They have forced our hand.

"Cassidy!" Elle exclaims, bursting into the room, breathless. "They've got the radios working again!"

I snap upright.

"Great!" I say.

I follow her down the hall, to the third level, where the offices and computer lab is. The hostages have been moved out of the compound and into an empty barracks building guarded by Mad Monks.

In the office room, Father Kareem is sitting on a chair directly across from the Intelligence Supervisor. His name is Hung Lee, and he is glaring with fierce animosity at Father Kareem. Blood dribbles from the sides of his mouth.

"Radios?" I say as I walk in.

Andrew looks up from a table filled with radios, computers and gadgets. He has that feverish glint in his eye – the look he gets when he is working on something complicated and difficult. It's the expression he has when he is in his element.

"Yeah," he says. "I started with an entirely new radio, and I had to tap into the signal and...you know what? Let's just say I fixed it and leave the details for another time."

Vera – who is sitting on the table – lets out a relieved sigh.

I take the receiver in my hand, my thumb hovering over the button.

"This thing will plug into every airwave from here to the bottom of California," Andrew says. "I reworked the radio tower on the top of the compound – that thing is a beast. I disabled Omega's satellite links and hooked up our stuff instead."

I pat him on the shoulder.

"Good job, soldier," I grin. "I knew I could count on you."

He shrugs, but Vera beams at him. Even with all of their bickering, they still love each other, and she is proud of him. I see it in her eyes every time she looks at him, and I am happy that they have learned to love each other in the middle of this devastation.

I press my thumb against the receiver and say, "Eagle's Nest, this Yankee Leader, over. Come in, Eagle's Nest."

I let go and listen for a response, but I hear nothing but static.

"Eagle's Nest," I say one more time. "This is Yankee Leader, come in. Over."

Still, no response. I try to get an answer for several minutes before I give up. Em enters the room, her lips set into a thin line. I hold the radio out to her.

"Tap in with the National Guard," I tell her. "Let them know that we need them down here."

She nods and picks up the radio.

"Gold Leader," she says, "this is Whiskey One. Please respond, over."

"Whiskey One, this is Gold Leader," the radio replies. A male voice. "Go ahead."

I nod, and Em goes ahead with her message for Colonel Wilcox, the commanding officer of the National

Guard. I haven't met the guy, but from what I hear, he's pretty easy to work with.

"What do we do if Omega comes back here and tries to take the base again?" Vera whispers.

"The National Guard will take care of it," I say. "That's why we're leaving them here – we're occupying this base."

Vera nods.

When Em is done relaying her orders, she turns to me.

"Done," she says. "National Guard forces will be here at approximately 1200 hours today."

Relief floods through me, and then the radio crackles.

"Yankee Leader, this is Eagle's Nest. We have received your transmission. Go ahead."

The voice is distinctly female, and I would recognize it anywhere: Arlene.

My heart jumps into my chest. A response!

"We read you, Eagle's Nest," I say. "We have taken Mendenhall. Repeat, we have taken Mendenhall with all of their packages and are returning to Gold Leader fully loaded."

"Copy that, Yankee Leader," Arlene replies. "How fully loaded are you talking?"

I look to Andrew for the correct radio codes – if Omega is listening, I don't want to give anything away. "Frank Sinatra," he mouths, giving me a thumbs up.

"We are fully loaded and we've got Frank Sinatra with us," I reply.

There is a moment of silence.

"Frank is with you," Arlene answers at last. "Good to hear. When can we expect Frank to perform?"

"As soon as possible," I reply. "No ETA at this time."

"Very well."

"What is your current status, Eagle's Nest?" I ask.

"We are alive and well," she replies. "Good to hear your voice, Yankee Leader."

"We're going radio silent, Eagle's Nest," I continue. "Use contacts with Gold Leader for further information."

"Over and out, Yankee Leader."

"Roger."

I put the radio down, a small smile on my face.

So. Arlene knows that we're headed back to California with nuclear submarines and seized Omega weaponry. What they *don't* know is that we have militias across the country fighting the same fight that we are.

I can't wait to tell her. I can't wait to tell *Chris*.

"So what now, Commander?" Em asks.

"We go back to Yukon City," I say. "And we take those ballistic subs back to California, and we hit Omega with everything we've got on the way."

She smiles.

Chapter Thirteen

2 Days Later, Yukon City, Port of Whittier, Alaska

Military Stronghold, S.S.B.N Peter

Yukon City. We are back.

The port is frigid. I shiver in the freezing wind, my hood pulled tightly around my face, my hands shoved into black gloves. The ballistic subs sit in the harbor, great, hulking black monsters peeking above the icy water. I stare at them, truly and honestly intimidated at the thought of descending into their bellies and diving into the depths of the sea.

The city is a flurry of activity. The National Guard is gone, and all that is left is a hollow shell of a town in the snow and the ice. Civilians who staged an attack on Begich Towers are corralled into the city park area, living in RVs and pop-up campers.

As for Mauve Bacardi...she is still in intensive care, deep in a coma. She may never wake up, and I can't say that I feel bad for her. Maybe I'm just hardened, or maybe I'm just mean. But the fact remains that she abused her power here in Yukon City, and without her around, our time in the city has been much more pleasant.

"Commander Hart." A stoic, older man with gray hair and cobalt eyes salutes me.

"You must be Captain Stanley," I say.

"Yes." He nods. "It will be a pleasure having you and your men onboard."

"Thank you. We appreciate your efforts."

"Same for you."

"If you'll excuse me, I have some duties to perform."

"Of course."

He walks away, and I wonder what his story is – how he ended up here.

The crews of the subs are ambling around the docks, talking and swapping jokes. They are eased and relaxed – the thought of getting into the metal monster doesn't scare them like it scares me.

I take a deep breath and tell myself to suck it up.

I am, after all, a commander. I can't let my men see me like this.

"You okay, Cassidy?" Margaret Young asks. She is standing next to me with Isabel. The young girl's pale blond hair is piled beneath a black beanie. She stares at the subs with an intensity that I have never seen in her before.

"Fine," I murmur. "Are *you* okay?"

"Well enough. We have survived to live another day."

I am grateful to God that the civilian coup did not count Margaret and Isabel among the casualties. When the uprising was happening, she and Isabel burrowed into the back closet in one of the penthouse apartments, curling up and waiting for hours until the gunfire and screaming stopped.

The fact that I was not here to protect them for Chris will plague me forever.

I cannot get rid of that guilt – not ever.

"I'm glad we're going back to California," Margaret says. "It's home."

"It always will be," I agree.

"And I miss my son."

I say nothing, because hey – I miss him too. But it's a little different.

"Why don't you guys go ahead and board," I say, clearing my throat. "Captain Stanley or one of the crewmen will be able to show you to your quarters."

"Are we going to kill everybody in California?" Isabel suddenly asks. She looks at me, her gaze hardened. "That's what Uriah told me."

I knit my brow.

"Uriah is wrong," I reply. "We're only fighting the enemy."

Margaret hauls a duffel bag over her shoulder.

"Let's go, honey," she murmurs.

She does not look at me as they move toward the sub, away from me.

God. Now Margaret is afraid of me, too. Who have I become?

When I turn around, I meet the steady, dark gaze of Uriah. He is standing there, still as a statue, frowning. I hadn't even realized he was here.

"You spying on me or something?" I quip, but the joke is forced.

"Just thinking," Uriah replies.

"About what?"

He doesn't answer. He walks closer and stops a couple of feet away from me, a muscle ticking in his jaw.

"You know," he says, his voice low. "We could stay here. Base our operations in Yukon City, and strike Omega when we *want* to. We'd be on the offensive for once. We could build a life here, together. We could –"

I take a step back, sensing the desperation in his voice. The longing.

"We're going back," I say. "California needs us."

"No. *Chris* needs us," Uriah replies, vitriol in his tone. "Otherwise we would stay here, you and me. And you know I'm right."

I stare at him, at the anguish in his expression. I see it then as I have never seen it before: heartbreak. Uriah loves me in a way I can never return, and that eats away at him like poison. I shake my head.

"We're not talking about this," I tell him. "Nobody's making you come back to California with me, but I know you, Uriah. Nobody's going to take you out of the fight – it's in your blood. You're a creature of war, you said so yourself."

From the edge of the pier, Vera, Manny, Cheng, Elle and Bravo begin arriving at last. My eyes dart to their moving forms and then back at Uriah. He doesn't flicker.

"We're both creatures of war," he argues. "And this constant return to California is going to kill us one of these days."

"Then that's the way it is," I say. "We'll have died for something worth fighting for."

I take a step forward and walk around him, heading straight toward my friends coming up the pier. Uriah does not move. He just remains in the same spot, staring at the subs in the harbor.

"Hey," he says.

I turn around. He meets my gaze.

"In the strategy room at the compound in Mendenhall," he goes on. "The mug shot of me. The one where I had been arrested."

"Yeah?" I reply.

"I killed men. A lot of them. Before the Collapse."

I raise my eyebrow, apprehensive.

"What kind of men?" I ask.

"Bad men. Men that burned my house, killed my dog, murdered my girlfriend." His black eyes flicker with a spark of fury. "It was a crime mob, even in the sticks, where I was from. This big, Russian mob ruled everything. And I was young, hotheaded. I thought I could take them – so I did. I got the ringleaders arrested."

"What happened then?" I ask.

"They put a price on my head," Uriah replies. "They found my house, beat me up, burned the house down, shot my dog and murdered my girlfriend." He closes his eyes. "Her name was Elena."

"That's a pretty name," I whisper.

"She was a pretty girl." He looks away. "It took me time to recover, physically and mentally. But when I did..." He rubs his chin and locks his eyes on mine. "I found them – the guys that did it. I killed them. All of them."

I can't believe what I'm hearing. Uriah...a murderer before the Collapse? I mean, yes, his victims were bad people...but *Uriah*? Should this surprise me, knowing his tendency toward killing? Probably not. But does that mean that I want to hear it? No, of course not.

"All of them?" I ask, my voice trembling.

"Yeah. I was a cop, Cassidy, and I killed them." He looks at the ground. "All twenty-three of them."

My eyes widen.

"God, Uriah. That's..."

"Insane?" he interrupts. "I know. I knew when I did it that it was the end of my life – but I didn't care. I was on a vigilante mission of justice." He laughs hollowly. "I was angry and broken, and I didn't care about the rest of my life. I even turned myself into the cops."

I stare at him, remembering a few years ago when a small-town police officer made headlines for massacring a group of Russian gang members. It was the hottest news in every newspaper and cable channel for at least two months.

I had been young, then. Maybe thirteen. I didn't pay attention to names or faces.

"Is your name really Uriah True?" I whisper.

He replies, "No."

I let this sink in, the gut-wrenching, soul-searing truth.

Then I say, "I don't want to know your real name."

Silence. I hear Elle's voice. They have almost reached us.

"I was being transported from a maximum-security prison cell to my court hearing the day the lights when out," Uriah continues. "The bus crashed, the driver was killed. I got out. I escaped the city. And when society collapsed...I got a chance to start over. I could do what I was good at, without consequences."

"Killing," I say.

He nods.

"How did you find the Freedom Fighters?" I ask.

"Your father," he replies. "He never told you, did he?"

I shake my head, afraid to hear the words that are about to leave his mouth.

"Ready to take the great plunge into the icy depths of the sea?" Manny cracks, walking up behind me, flashing a wry grin. "I know how much you love being contained in tight spaces."

"Shut up," I say, startled out of the conversation. "I'm ready enough."

Great timing, Manny. Great timing.

Uriah's lips are pressed into a thin line, and I can see that our conversation is over. The knowledge that he has just handed to me churns in my stomach like a hurricane...Uriah True...a mass murderer?

But he only killed the people who hurt him. Criminals and thugs.

Does that make it right? Is it wrong that I'm judging Uriah for killing people before the Collapse – as if the devastation of civilization wiped the slate clean and gave us new rules for killing people? Am I trying to justify what he did because I have killed so many people myself?

The people I kill are the enemy. I am acting in self-defense. It's different.

"You okay?" Elle asks, regarding me coolly.

"Fine," I reply quickly. "Let's get out of here."

I move forward without looking at her. I am sure that the shock of Uriah's revelation is obvious on my face. I need to get away from it – think about something else. We walk to the sub and Captain Stanley is standing there, his blue uniform pristine and his jaw set.

"Welcome aboard the *U.S.S. Peter*, Commander Hart," he says.

"Thank you," I reply.

We walk up the gangplank to the hatch, the dark water lapping the sides of the sub beneath our feet. Elle and Bravo are directly behind me. I hear Cheng say cheerfully, "Let's hope we don't all die."

Manny laughs and replies, "I gotta say, this is the one thing I've never done: taken a ride in a submarine. And a ballistic missile sub, at that!"

We duck into the hatch and climb a long flight of metal stairs. The sub is lit from within, dimly illuminated with orange and white lights. It smells like ocean water and recirculated air. When we hit the first level, the first thing I notice is that it is not as small as I was afraid it would be. Even Manny and Uriah have enough headspace to stand up straight. There is a long row of doorways and hatches stretching straight down a hallway before us, and behind us, another flight of stairs continues to a lower level.

Crewman are scurrying through the halls, curiously glancing at us as we follow Captain Stanley down the hallway. As we walk, I am barely aware of the slight movement of the sub as it bobs in the harbor.

Good thing I don't get seasick...not as far as I'm aware, anyway.

We walk and walk, climbing down one more flight of metal steps and reaching a hallway with narrow doors and harsh white light.

"These will be your quarters while you are onboard," Captain Stanley announces. "You can house two crewmen per room, so choose your roommate and carry on." He points to the left. "Down this hall and to the right is Command Control, and beyond that is the Wardroom. CPO living quarters are at the helm of the sub. If you need to locate me at any time, Command Control will be able to help you out."

"Where's the food?" Cheng asks, unceremoniously pointing out what we are all thinking.

"The Wardroom *is* the mess hall," Captain Stanley explains. "You will take your meal rotation at 0600 every morning, lunch at 1200 and dinner at 1800. Understood?"

"Perfectly, Captain Stanley," I say. "Thank you."

"When we reach our target, you will be notified and summoned to Command Control," he goes on, looking directly at me.

"Sounds good."

"I will even go so far as to say that in all the years that this submarine has been active duty, we have never had women onboard." His gaze flicks first to Elle, then Vera and back to me. "I would encourage you to stay in your cabins as much as possible."

And with that, he is gone, disappearing into the bowels of the sub, probably off to stand in Command Control.

"What, does he think I'm some delicate flower?" Vera gripes. "Like I'm going to stay in my cabin the entire time just because my presence might upset the *men*? You've got be kidding –"

"He's just trying to be helpful," I tell Vera. "Calm down."

"Whatever."

I open the door to the first cabin. There are two bunks attached to the wall, along with a tiny bathroom and sink in the corner. It's incredibly small, but it's better than nothing. I walk in, plop my backpack on the floor and Vera follows me.

"What's up, roomie?" I ask, smiling faintly.

"Don't get creepy with me, Hart." She turns away, but I can tell that she is trying not to smile. Elle and Bravo get their own cabin, while Cheng and Manny snag another one. Andrew rooms with Uriah. Once I have secured my gear, I leave the cabin behind and venture into the hall. The crew is still getting ready for departure.

"So much for staying in your cabin as much as possible," Vera calls after me, poking her head out the cabin door.

"Come with me," I say. "Don't you want to see this thing submerge?"

Vera shakes her head, looking queasy, and then shuts the cabin door.

I guess I can see her point. I'm not crazy about being contained in this sub, either, but I'll be better off embracing it than pretending it's not happening. So I follow Captain Stanley's directions and find Command Control, ducking into a hatch and taking a step into a large room filled with glowing computer screens.

Crewmen are sitting at chairs around every screen, their hands on controls and button-boards, chattering into headsets. Captain Stanley raises an eyebrow when I walk in.

"Cabin fever already?" he asks.

"I want to see this thing submerge," I reply.

He almost smiles.

Emphasis on *almost*.

"Very well," he replies. "Have you ever been on a submarine before?"

"No, sir."

"Then you are about to be educated, Commander Hart."

Several minutes pass. The control room is full of concentrated, controlled activity. I place my hand on the metal wall and take a deep breath.

Just think. In a couple of days, you will be back in California, with Chris. This submarine ride will be well worth it...not just for you, but for the entire militia.

At some point, the hatch above is closed by the crewman and the submarine comes alive. I feel a shiver of fearful anticipation. Now I am *literally* in the belly of the beast. I look at the screens mounted on the wall. I can see the surface of the water as the sub pulls away from the harbor. I feel the movement of the vessel now, and I tell myself to breathe evenly.

Five minutes pass, then fifteen, and then twenty. We put more and more distance between us and Whittier's port. We push out farther and farther, the water foaming and frothing around the visible strip of submarine at the surface – all five hundred and sixty feet of hulking metal and machine.

One of the officers climbs down a ladder from the level above. He is young, his hair bright red, freckles dotting every inch of skin on his face.

"Ready for dive, ready for dive," he says.

"Ready for dive, aye, sir," another seaman responds from the control panel.

"Quartermaster, sounding," Captain Stanley says.

The Quartermaster – a burly man with bushy eyebrows – reads off a long string of depth numbers.

"Very well, Officer Greene," Captain Stanley says. "Submerge the ship."

"Yes, sir." Officer Greene flips a switch and a mild klaxon rings through the ship. "Dive, dive," he says into the radio. The siren continues to wail and he repeats the warning over and over again.

And then we begin to dive. I clutch the wall as tightly as I can, staring at the screens. Water begins to wash over the submarine and I can feel the pressure change in the cabin as the ballast tanks fill with water, using the weight of the ocean itself to submerge the vessel. We start sinking into the sea. I can feel the slow downward movement of the sub as we plow through the sea, the negative buoyancy taking us down, down.

"The deck's awash," someone calls out.

Down we go. My ears pop. I yawn and the pressure is released. I continually move my jaw and yawn to release the pressure as we continue to submerge deeper and deeper, disappearing from the surface of the earth and plunging into the black, icy depths of the unforgiving ocean.

***

The crushing deep of the sea does little to help me sleep. It's maybe 0200, and I am lying wide awake on the top bunk, Vera sleeping on the bottom. A dim orange light glows in the corner of the room. I can hear the creak of the sub and the low rumble of the engine. I sit up in a cold sweat, imagining a hole puncturing the shell of the sub, the pressure of the water immediately killing all of us.

Come on, Cassidy. This submarine is well protected, and so are the others.

I swing my legs over the side of the bed and clutch the gold chain around my neck, kissing it lightly. If Chris were here, I'm sure he would know what to say. I would feel safe and secure. Besides, the water is where Chris has always felt most at home. I often forget that. We have only ever fought on dry land...but Chris's background as a SEAL makes him conducive to water operations.

I wish I could have seen Chris when he was my age, a young gun in the Navy. I wonder if we would have been friends then. If we would have fallen in love. If he

274

had known me, would we have gotten married? Or would he have married Jane instead?

It's strange to think of Chris's late wife, to know that there was another woman before me. Not that I'm bitter – she was murdered, and I can't imagine what that must have been like for Chris.

Who knows? All that matters is that I love Chris right now.

I slip out of my bunk and keep my gun on my belt, as well as my knife. I open the cabin door and step into the hall, still brightly lit. I wander down the hallway, most of the sub silent. There are still a lot of men on duty. This vessel is manned by at least one hundred and fifty crewmen, although I suspect that the number is lower right now. All five of these subs are carrying militiamen.

"Hey, Commander."

Em Davis is standing in the hallway leading to the Wardroom, looking worn and weary. Her dog, India, is sitting beside her leg.

"Em," I say. "You okay?"

"Couldn't sleep. You?"

"Same."

"This sub is freaking me out," she says, and grins.

"It's a little disconcerting, yeah."

Silence. Then, "Thanks for letting me come with you."

I shrug. "Thanks for coming."

"I want to do my part in this war," she goes on. "I really do. I left for a while, but now I'm ready to come back, just like you."

I lick my lips.

"These weapons we're going to unleash on the coastline," I say. "We'll be killing more Omega soldiers at once than ever before. It's kind of scary, you know? But necessary."

"Very." Em looks grave. "They killed my family. Omega, I mean. They killed them all...every last one. My two brothers, my parents, my grandparents. They even killed our stupid goldfish."

"I'm so sorry," I tell her, and I mean it.

"Don't be. We've all lost someone."

She's right about that.

"What about your family?" she asks. "What happened to them?"

"My dad was KIA," I reply. "My mom...I don't know. I haven't seen her since before the Collapse. Heard she moved to San Francisco. If that was true, then the chances of her surviving the Omega forces there were slim. She's probably dead, too."

Saying that out loud is sobering. I feel a deep wash of sadness.

It's as if I'm finally acknowledging the death of my parents.

"That's too bad," Em says. "Sucks to live in this world these days."

"Not always," I whisper. "There are still good people left."

"A few."

"The militias have a *lot* of good people."

"Yeah," she agrees. "I can't argue with you there. I mean, Margaret Young and Isabel are nice people, I'm glad they're here."

I say, "Thank you for watching out for them when I was in Mendenhall."

Em shrugs.

"How long have you had your dog?" I ask.

"Since she was a pup," Em replies, and there is a hint of pride in her voice. "I was training to be a K-9 handler in the Marines, once upon a time. I was stationed at Camp Pendleton before the Collapse. My dog had never seen active combat before Omega came. We learned quickly."

"She's beautiful," I remark.

"She's my best friend."

"If all of this ends," I say, "what are you going to do? Stay with the militias?"

"Fighting is what I do best," she tells me. "Don't you feel the same way?"

I rake my hair back with my hand.

"Yeah," I admit. "I guess I do."

Chapter Fourteen

The Wardroom is crowded. I mean, in high school, I thought my house was crowded – and I only shared it with one person: my dad. But here in the submarine, the christened mess hall is filled with more bodies than I think is humanly possible. Seamen and militiamen alike are crammed into this room, complete with three tables, each packed with as many chairs as possible. Each person takes a plate, goes to the cafeteria window, receives their rations and then sits down – either with a mug of hot coffee or a tall glass of ice water.

I am sitting in the corner with Em Davis and Elle. Their dogs are in their cabins – there's just not enough space for canines in this room. Manny is crammed between two seamen. His long, gangly legs are smashed under the table, and I can see the irritation on his face as he tries to take a swig of coffee, but he's bumped in the arm by the man beside him.

"Sorry, mate," the guy says.

Manny just glares.

I look down at the remains of my meal: meat and potatoes with gravy. I drain the last drop of coffee from my mug. Vera sits next to Andrew across from me. She has barely touched her food, and her pale face is a muted shade of green.

Seasickness.

"I think I'll get her back to her room," Andrew says, sighing.

"I'm *fine*," she hisses.

"Take her to see the medic," I say. "He'll give her some seasickness meds."

Andrew nods and helps Vera out of her seat. She follows him out, muttering under her breath until they leave the room. I make a mental note to check on Margaret and Isabel later...they have been eating in their cabins, the two of them both plagued by seasickness, as well. I can't help but laugh a little at Vera's exit, and then I turn my attention to Uriah. He is sitting by himself in the corner of the room, surrounded by strangers. And all he does is drink coffee and watch me.

"Lieutenant True is very intense," Em says.

"Hmm? Oh, yeah, I guess," I reply absently.

"He's always watching you. It's almost like he doesn't care about anyone else."

"That's not true. Uriah's just...conflicted."

I clutch the coffee mug, nausea rising in my throat. Am I actually afraid of Uriah? He revealed his past to me, yes. But does that make him any different than the Uriah I know and care about? The Uriah who has faithfully fought by my side since the days of guerilla warfare in the high mountains?

The klaxon wails. I snap upright. The siren is followed by: "Commander Hart, report to Command Control."

A stone drops to the pit of my stomach. We have reached target position.

I stand and walk out of the room – the eye of every seaman on me as I go. Elle and Em trail after me. Manny slams his food down on the table.

"Thank God – an excuse to leave this tin can!" he exclaims.

He storms out of the Wardroom and follows us into the hallway.

"We must be in position, then?" he asks me.

I don't reply. I am too busy thinking about what lies ahead – the eradication of Omega's presence from the coastline. By the time we reach Command Control, I am almost shaking with nervous anticipation.

And then Uriah is there, standing behind me, his breath hot against my neck.

"This is it," he says, low.

I take a step away.

"Yeah," I mutter.

"Commander Hart," Captain Stanley says, raising an eyebrow. "You brought an audience."

"These are my platoon leaders," I say. "I want them here."

He nods, clearly not in the mood to argue with me.

"We're in position," he says. "We're waiting for the order."

"Who gives the order?" Elle asks, folding her arms across her chest.

"Commander Hart," Captain Stanley replies, looking at me. "Normally, the release of such a weapon is issued from a civilian to the military – such as the President of the United States to the Pentagon. But these are dire times, and this is a para-military operation. Commander Hart, as a representative of the Pacific Northwest Alliance, this gives you the authority to give the order."

I swallow a lump in my throat. Of course it has to be me. It's not like these subs are linked to the military at home. This is our mission – and ours alone.

The internal war within me is powerful – a hurricane of emotions, of guilt, of bitterness, of sadness.

Here I am, able to pull the trigger on Omega at last – the ultimate act of vengeance, an idea that keeps me awake at night and bleeds into my every breathing moment.

So why is this so hard for me?

I can't do it, I think. *I don't want to be the one to do this.*

"Cassidy," Manny says. He puts an arm around my shoulders, lowering his voice. "This is not just your decision. This is *our* decision, my girl. We will all carry it with us – this is not something that you have to bear alone, my girl."

I look up at him, tears blurring my vision.

"Thank you," I whisper.

He nods, squeezes my shoulders, and then lets go.

This is the moment. This is it.

"Captain Stanley," I say evenly. "You have a green light."

He nods.

"May God forgive us," I say quietly, and for the first time since I have met Father Kareem, I grasp the importance of his reliance on his faith. There is simply no other way to deal with something of this magnitude.

I blink my tears away. This is a decision that had to be made – an order that had to be given.

"Weapons system is in condition," Officer Greene says, as monotone as ever.

"Key code is valid, roger," Captain Stanley responds.

More chatter, more codes. More radio call signs and communications with the sister subs traveling with us.

"SSBN-627, this is SSBN-939," the radio crackles.

Elle raises an eyebrow.

"SSBN-939 is one of the other subs," I say. "It's the *U.S.S. Stinger.*"

"We copy you, SSBN-939," Captain Stanley replies.

"All launch prerequisites have been met," they reply.

"SSBN-627 concurs."

There is a long beat of silence. I look at the computer screens and I see a sonar readout. I also spot a digital map on one of the screens, and I recognize San Francisco Bay immediately.

"You brought this on yourself," I whisper.

San Francisco, once so beautiful. Now, nothing but a collection of devastated rubble and thousands of Omega soldiers, infecting the city like a colony of termites.

Elle gives me a sad look, but says nothing.

"SSBN-627, you have permission to fire," the radio crackles.

I inhale.

"Missile away," Captain Stanley says.

I exhale.

The entire submarine shakes slightly as the ballistic missile empties from its chamber, plunging through the water, toward the surface. When it breaks the surface, a fiery propulsion explodes beneath it and drives it into the sky, toward its target on land.

I place a hand on my chest.

We've done it. We've really, *truly* done it.

"Missile is on trajectory," Officer Green says.

Elle's fingers are pressed against her lips, and she's staring intently at the map of San Francisco. Manny is stone silent.

"Missile is on trajectory," Officer Greene repeats.

He says this several times. As the minutes tick by, I pray under my breath that God will somehow find it in his heart to forgive us for this war, for this killing. For this horrific measure that we have taken in order to secure our freedom and future victory.

"We have a confirmed hit," Officer Green says suddenly. "The missile has detonated in the harbor, sir."

Elle releases a breath and Uriah's fists tighten.

"So it's done, then," Elle whispers. "We've struck back."

I don't reply.

Captain Stanley turns to me, his face as expressionless as ever.

"The *U.S.S. Peter* is capable of holding twenty-four ballistic missiles at one time," he says. "I suppose what I'm saying, Commander, is that we have plenty of insurance on board."

"You want to launch more at the city," I say.

He raises his hands.

"It's your call, Commander," he replies.

I consider this – one or two more missiles would make absolutely certain that not a single Omega trooper within fifty miles survived the biochemical weapon.

"Do it," Uriah says.

I meet Captain Stanley's gaze. I nod.

He dips his head, and then he picks up the radio, and we start all over again.

***

We are up all day, into the late hours of the night. As our sub fleet moves down the coastline, we wreak destructive chaos on our home state for the sake of driving the enemy out. We launch missiles in San Francisco, San Jose, Monterey, San Luis Obispo, San Simeon, Santa Barbara, Ventura...any place where Omega troops have congregated in large numbers. There is no shortage of Omega occupation, and between the five subs headed south, we have no shortage of missiles.

And so we empty our stores of them, launching the potent, poisonous weapons at the towns along the coastline where we know Omega is keeping the bulk of their invading armies.

Silent and stealthy as we are, we have no radio contact with the militias or the outside world. Our best weapon is our silence, as Captain Stanley tells me, and we will not know the extent of the damage we have done until we surface in San Diego.

It is not until we reach Los Angeles that the morbidity of our mission really sets in on me. Los

Angeles – my home. I know that it has been hit before with a chemical weapon by Omega...but now, I am the one who is giving the order to hit it again.

My only hope is that if there are any survivors left there, that they will somehow survive this attack. But my common sense is louder than my hopeful nature; I know that Omega has completely taken over the urban city. Anything left needs to be destroyed.

When we have launched missiles at Los Angeles and Long Beach, our destructive assault finally ends. I clutch the wall, emotionally spent, my mouth and throat dry.

"Mission accomplished," Elle whispers, and she turns away, slipping into the hall.

"So it's done, then," Manny says. He puts his hand on my shoulder. "It was a necessary purge, my girl. There was no other way."

I know that he is right – Manny is pretty much *always* right.

But that doesn't make this any easier, not really. I talk to Captain Stanley for a few more minutes and then turn to Manny and Uriah, who are still staring balefully at the computer screens.

I feel odd and detached.

At last, we have had a victory against the Omegan forces, and yet we still feel hollow and spent. And I think I know why – it is because we sacrificed so much of our humanity for this war. We defend ourselves because we fear the scourge of Omega. I guess, in a way, that fear has really driven us to come this far. After all, without fear, there can be no courage.

"Let's get out of here," Uriah mutters.

We leave Command Control, head back to the Wardroom, and all of us – Captain Stanley included – grab a hot mug of coffee and gather around the table.

We enjoy our first moment of true peace in months.

Chapter Fifteen

U.S.S. Peter (SSBN 627 – Ohio Class)

San Diego, California

It is early morning when we arrive in San Diego. I sit on the edge of the bottom bunk, waiting for Vera to finish using the bathroom. My backpack is slung over my shoulder, along with my rifle, and I focus on breathing evenly.

Almost done. Almost home.

Yes, I have never been to San Diego before. But the truth has always been clear to me: my home is wherever Chris is. Always. And when I am on dry land again, the first thing I will do is make radio contact with Sector 27 and check in with him.

"You done yet?" I ask, impatient.

"I'm working on it! Rome wasn't built in a day, geez," Vera shoots back.

I roll my eyes and stand up, leaning on the wall, anxious to leave. We are maybe ten minutes away from emerging from the watery depths of the ocean. Ten minutes until we surface. Ten minutes until we are back on dry land, and I step foot on Californian turf once more.

Finally, Vera emerges from the bathroom, her platinum-blond hair pulled into a slick ponytail, a baseball cap snugly resting on her head.

"Happy now?" she snaps.

"Yeah. Let's go."

We leave the cabin and head toward Command Control one more time, where I know Captain Stanley will be. When we duck inside, the rest of my platoon is already there.

"See?" I whisper. "Everybody was waiting on you."

"Beauty takes time," she replies.

Of course, I know she's joking, but still. Annoying.

"Welcome back to the Golden State," Captain Stanley says. And this time, there is the slight hint of a smile on his lips.

Miracles can happen, I suppose.

We all watch with bated breath as the ballast tanks blow their water and fill with air, pulling the submarine up through the water. The rising sensation quakes in my stomach, but I feel myself smiling anyway.

As the submarine reaches the surface, it rises above the water with a tremendous burst of motion, throwing us all forward. I grab Uriah's arm to steady myself as the sub hits the top of the harbor, and then the screens in Command Control register daylight.

Bright, beautiful, pure daylight.

After being stuck in the barren winter solstice of Alaska, it looks like heaven. I let go of Uriah's arm and step away from him, focused on the activity in the control room. The *Peter* plows through the waves. Nervous anticipation pools in my stomach.

Will Chris be waiting for us to arrive? By now, we have made radio contact with the naval air station, and they know we are coming in to dock.

"This is going to be different," Manny says, turning to me. "This time, when we get off this thing, we're the victorious ones."

I nod, slightly. He's right...and I'm not sure if that revelation is calming yet.

As we come into the docking area, the sub slows down. I leave Command Control and walk to the stairway that leads to the main hatch, tapping the strap of my backpack. Uriah is right behind me. I turn to him.

"What?" I ask.

"We never got to finish talking," he replies. "In Alaska, we were interrupted."

"I don't want to know anything else," I say, firmly. "I mean it."

"You think your dad didn't know who I was?" Uriah presses. "I met him in the city, Cassidy. He recognized me – he's a cop, for the love of God. He knew *exactly* who I was and what I'd done."

I stare at him.

"He never told me this," I say.

"He gave me a chance to start over," Uriah says, his eyes reddening. Tears? "He believed in me when no one else did. I went with him to your cabin, Cassidy, all that time ago. We started the Freedom Fighters together. We helped build Camp Freedom."

I feel as if someone has taken a knife and twisted it in my heart.

How could my father keep this secret from me? How could *Uriah* keep this secret from me? They knew each other since the beginning of the Collapse?

"I fell in love with the idea of finding you before I even met you," Uriah whispers. "I wanted to be the one to rescue you, to prove to your father that I could be a better man than the one I was when I killed those men."

I swallow.

"Uriah – "

"But you found *me*," he interjects. "*You* changed *me*. You showed me morality again, how to fight for something *worth* fighting for. Cassidy, I owe everything to you, and to your father. Like it or not, we're bonded, you and me."

I run a hand through my unruly red hair and shake my head.

"You should have told me a long time ago," I say.

"My past is not something I tell just anyone."

"I'm not just *anyone*." I level my gaze. "We're friends, you and me. We trust each other. You should have told me." I take a deep breath. "But it's in the past, now. Whatever you did back then...it doesn't matter anymore. You're Uriah True today, right now, and until the day you die. Understood?"

He says nothing.

"Don't think ill of me, Cassidy," he says quietly. "Just remember, I never did anything without you in mind."

I frown, just as the klaxon wails on the submarine, the whistle blows, and the radio crackles with orders from Command Control. Seamen scuttle around the hallways and voices echo off the walls. Elle runs down the hall, an excited grin plastered across her face. Cheng follows behind her, as always. I'm starting to think that boy is her permanent shadow.

"Home, home, home," Elle is muttering.

Two seamen climb the metal stairwell and the hatch pops open with a loud hiss and a bolt of bright sunlight. My eyes water from the sudden influx of light. I feel the warmth of it on my skin and take a deep breath.

Ocean air. Thank God.

I hurry up the steps, my boots clanging on the metal staircase, emerging on the top of the sub.

Coronado Naval Air Station.

The sun sears my vision and the wind from the bay cuts into my cheeks. But compared to the frigid temperatures of Alaska, this is almost sweltering weather. The harbor is huge and blue behind me. A massive blue bridge spans the space between Coronado Island and San Diego. The city itself is in relatively good condition. A few buildings have fallen, but the bulk of the urban skyline is still intact. Coast Guard Cutters patrol the water, and in the distance, warships are guarding the coastline.

I walk down the gangplank, onto the dock. To our left, a mighty aircraft carrier is docked, being serviced by dozens of Naval seamen. A road runs parallel to the dock, busy with military vehicles and foot traffic. Buildings dot the perimeter, and to the right, two large air hangars are sparkling in the early morning light.

A fleet of military Apache helicopters sit on the tarmac – there are at least two dozen of them. I hear the powerful blades of a Blackhawk and watch it thunder above our heads.

I smile. Here, in the middle of the military might of the United States Navy, I feel safe.

"This beats Alaska, any day," Manny exclaims, stepping onto the dock. "Can you believe this weather? I'll have to shed a few layers if you ask…"

He trails off. He, like me, has spotted the welcoming party at the end of the dock. It is a small group of Naval Airmen, and at the front of the crowd, Arlene Costas is waiting. She is wearing blue fatigues and a white shirt. Her loose, gray hair is braided down her back.

What is she doing here? Why is Arlene *here?*

Fear of the unknown races through me. What happened to Sector 27?

If Arlene is here, why isn't Chris here?

Oh, please no. God, no.

Sick terror swirls in the pit of my stomach, just as Margaret Young and Isabel climb off the sub behind me. I turn to Margaret and see the same look on her face: fear. Where is Chris?

Manny seems frozen for a moment, unsure of what to do.

"Go," I whisper.

He looks at me, genuinely lost. But he doesn't have to make the first move. For the first time since I have known Arlene, I see her *beam* with happiness. She runs forward and throws herself at Manny, locking her arms around his neck. She is crying, and Manny swings her around in a circle, laughing and grinning like a silly schoolboy.

I stand there and watch them, tears burning my vision. I swallow and straighten my shoulders. I don't want people to see me cry, not right now.

"I was afraid I'd never see you again," Arlene sniffles. "Dear God, you crazy old man. I can't believe you found your way home this time."

"I always do, my dear," Manny replies. "I always do."

"Arlene!" Elle says. She runs down the dock and embraces her aunt warmly. Bravo trots alongside her, tail bobbing back and forth.

Vera and Andrew walk hand in hand up the dock. Uriah watches the entire scene wordlessly. I look at the welcoming party at the docks, my heart sinking.

Chris is not among them.

"Where is he?" Margaret whispers, paling.

"Is he dead?" Isabel exclaims.

Margaret chokes on a sob.

"Isabel," I say. "No, of course not."

But the tremor in my voice tells the truth.

"Arlene," I exclaim.

She wraps me into a warm hug – surprising me. I gently return the gesture. Her eyes shine with tears. "Cassidy Hart," she says. "What have you done?"

I raise my eyebrows.

"Sorry?" I say.

"Everything has changed," she replies.

She pulls away, smoothing her hair. Straightening her spine.

"I guess you wouldn't know yet," she says.

"Know *what*?" I press.

She says, "Sector 27 no longer exists."

"What happened?" I ask, struggling to remain in control of the raging emotions in my head. "When we talked on the radio you said you were fine!"

"We were. It all happened in a single night. Omega attacked, of course. We couldn't hold them off, there were too many. They were trapping us inside the

303

desert mountain." She shakes her head. "There were just *too many* of them. So we retreated, and Commander Young ordered a self-destruct of the base."

I inhale.

"Where's Chris?" I ask quietly, terrified of her answer.

"That's not all," she says, carefully ignoring my question. "The biochemical weapons that you dropped on the coastline on your way down..."

"Spit it out, woman!" Vera exclaims, flushed.

"They were effective, for the most part," Arlene says, looking away. "But many of Omega's forces have settled in the Central Valley, away from the coastlines, sponging off the agricultural workers there. They're stealing the food and water supplies to feed their army."

"They've gone inland," I say, simply.

"Yes."

"And the biochemical weapons? The sarin gas?"

"The missiles that you deployed effectively destroyed Omega's forces in San Francisco, Monterey and Los Angeles." At this, she smiles a little. "It's the first ray of hope we've had in a long time. But the fight is far from over."

I feel relief – but only for a moment.

"Arlene," I say again, firmer. "Where is *Chris*? And don't you *dare* lie to me."

She looks at me.

"G Avenue," she whispers. "He's at home."

"*Home*?"

"You'll find him there."

"He's *here*?"

"Yes, Cassidy. He's here."

I look around.

"I need a car," I reply.

"I'll drive you," Uriah volunteers.

"No," I reply. "I'll go alone."

Arlene gestures to the Jeep sitting on the side of the road. She hands me the keys.

"Take my vehicle," she says. And then, "Good luck."

What is that supposed to mean?

I don't even say goodbye, and I definitely don't look back. I jog down the dock, past the crowd of people gathered to see the infamous Freedom Fighters, and throw my gear into the Jeep. The vehicle is open, without a roof or windows. I jam the key into the ignition and the car rumbles to life. My heart skips a beat and I speed down the road, leaving my platoon and the submarine and the harbor behind me.

I stop at the gate of the naval base and ask for directions to G Avenue. The men there help me out, but not without asking questions like "Are you *the* Commander Hart?" or "What you did with the missiles was a godsend, ma'am. Knocked Omega right off their feet."

I nod, say thank you, get the information I need, and then screech onto the roads outside the Naval Base. I see civilians here. Some of them are sweeping the gutters, others are gathering trash. A small shopping center has been renamed "THE TRADING SQUARE."

Men, women and children are milling around large stands and tents, trading food and clothing for valuable items like medicine and car parts.

I flit past. The air is warm and fresh, and the streets are incredibly clean. Apartment buildings and condominiums are crammed close together, white-washed and red-tiled. I can see that before the Collapse, this place was probably a very expensive location to live.

It takes me a long time, but I eventually find my way through neighborhoods of palm trees, magenta bougainvillea vines, shady trees and tropical flower gardens. I find G Avenue, and I pull the Jeep to the curb.

There are many houses here – all of them are gorgeous beach homes, neat and tidy. And, by the looks of it, probably extremely pricey. I hop out, bringing my rifle with me, and look around. The street is pretty quiet. All of the front lawns are dead, but most of the flowers and gardens are still flourishing.

There is an armored Humvee parked in front of a blue house with white trim. It is the only military

vehicle on the entire block, and I instantly know –
without a doubt – that this is where I will find Chris.

Don't be nervous. Just do this.

I cross the street and walk through the gate, up
the front steps and stop at the front door. It's wide open,
with only a flimsy screen door keeping me from
entering. I touch the handle. Unlocked.

"Chris?" I call.

I open the door and step inside. It's cool. The
floors are dark wood, and the walls are painted white. I
walk past a dining room table, through a shadowy
kitchen filled with boxes of dishes. In the living room,
there is one couch facing a white fireplace. Dusty
pictures line the top of the mantle.

This is where I find him.

He is sitting on the couch, his hands folded,
staring at the fireplace. His hair is pulled tight, his beard
is trimmed short. His electric green eyes find mine in
the reflection of the mirror on the wall.

"Chris," I say.

My heart is thundering my chest.

He slowly stands, turning and meeting my gaze, a storm of emotions on his face.

"I knew you'd come here to find me," he says.

"Why didn't you meet me at the dock?" I ask, my voice trembling. "Didn't you want to see me?"

"Of course I did. I just wanted it to be private." He doesn't move. "Are you okay?"

"Yeah. I'm fine. You?"

He nods.

There is a long silence. The tension between us is so thick – so heavy – that I could cut it with a knife.

"This is *your* house," I say, grim realization setting in. "This is the house you shared with Jane."

"Yes," he answers.

His muscles tense beneath the tight black shirt he wears tucked into his blue fatigues. He is tall and towering, more of a Navy SEAL now than I have ever seen him before.

"Why did you come here?" I ask. "Why did you want to meet me here?"

Something sick and dreadful festers in my stomach.

What is he trying to tell me?

"I wanted you to see," he says. "This is where I found Jane, dead. Right here, on the floor." He points to the carpet, a white area rug stained with dark spots. "Nobody even bothered to get the blood out of the floor."

I flinch.

"Why are you showing me this?" I ask.

"Because this is what my relationships are like," he tells me, swallowing hard. "The people I love die, or leave me. I do it to them – I get them killed, Cassie. It's what I *do*. And you...you would follow me into the gates of hell because you love me, so that you get killed and I'm left here to mourn for you."

"You're trying to get rid of me," I state, incredulous. Hot, acidic tears slip down my cheeks. "You're trying to scare me away."

"No," Chris replies. "You're a fighter, now. You know how this works."

"Yeah, I do."

"I just want you to realize that all of this" – he gestures to the space between us – "could be over in an instant, especially now."

"What's your *point,* Christopher?" I demand, using his full name.

He draws his eyebrows together, stepping closer.

"I've lost one wife," he tells me. "I don't want to lose you, too. So don't take this lightly."

"Chris, that doesn't make sense."

Chris pulls something from his pocket. It's gold in this lighting, glimmering dimly from the sunshine coming through the window.

"This is my class ring," he says. "I gave it to Jeff, before he died. You remember."

I nod. Yes, I remember.

"It's the best I've got," he says. He steps closer and touches my cheek. "Cassidy, will you marry me?"

I stare at him.

"What?" I gasp, shocked.

"Will you, Cassidy Hart, marry me?" A slight smile touches his lips, and he holds the ring higher. "Please?"

"Are you…serious?" I say, blinking.

"I'm as serious as I've ever been."

"But all of this…this talk about loss and death and – "

"I want you to be sure that you know what you're getting into."

I look at him, anger flashing in my eyes.

"If you think I don't know that already, then you don't know *me*," I say.

Chris nods, never taking his eyes from my face.

"You're right," he says. "I'm sorry."

Silence.

"So...?" he asks. "Will you?"

Something blossoms in my chest in this moment – something free, something pure. Something sweet and exciting. It's love, it's the giddy young girl inside of me, the love-struck teenager, the hopeless romantic buried deep beneath the layers of a tough exterior.

"Yes," I whisper. "Of course. There is no one else."

Chris laughs, and two tears escape his eyes, streaming down his face. He slips the heavy gold ring on my finger and a soft laugh bubbles out of me. I meet his gaze.

"I love you, Cassidy Hart," he says. "Until death do us part, and beyond."

"Same," I reply. "Always."

I wrap my arms around his neck, standing on the toes of my boots. Chris's strong arms hold me close to his chest. He kisses me, and it is the longest, surest kiss we have ever shared. It makes up for every heartache, every separation, every argument, every disappointment that we have ever had. His tears mix with mine and I taste their salty residue on my lips.

"What does marriage look like in the apocalypse, anyway?" I grin, kissing his cheek, his chin, his neck. "How do people do it now?"

"I don't know," he replies, spinning me around the room. "I don't care. I just love you, and I want to do this. For real. Both of us. It's about time."

I laugh again, wrapped in his strong embrace. I never want to leave again. Ever.

Chris slips his hand behind my back, pulling me close, his other hand flat against the wall. I fit my lips against his, the familiar scent of coffee and leather filling my senses. When I smell it, I am home. I am with Chris, and I am with the one person in the world who I can trust unconditionally.

I'm marrying Chris Young, I think. *I never thought we would do this.*

"It's so good to see you, Cassie," he smiles. "I missed you, you have no idea. I know I don't always say it, but having you around is the best part of my life. Without you, I'm apparently a real pain in the ass...at least that's what Arlene says."

"She's probably right." But I'm grinning.

"So how do you want to do this?" he asks. "Church wedding? Elope?"

"We can't elope, Chris. We're fighting a war."

"Yeah, well. I like to keep my options open."

"I don't know. I don't care. I just want to marry you."

"You're my kind of woman," he jokes.

Bam, bam, bam.

Someone bangs on the door. Chris frowns, but he doesn't remove his hand from my waist.

"Commander Young?"

I recognize the voice. Lieutenant Devin May, Chris's old Navy SEAL buddy, and a friend from our time in Monterey. He walks inside. He's nearly as tall as Chris, and just as powerful. His hair is shaved closed to the scalp, but today, he is as pale as a sheet.

"Lieutenant May," I say, smiling. "It's nice to see you again."

"Commander Hart," he replies, stony, barely even looking at me. "Chris, we gotta get out."

I raise my eyebrows – Devin has never been this coarse.

"What are you talking about, Devin?" Chris asks.

Somewhere on the island, a siren wails. It is a loud, screeching sound. I look to Chris, alarmed. "What is it?" I ask.

"Omega," Devin replies. "They're sending a nuke our way."

My eyes widen, and terror renders me motionless.

"*What?*" I breathe.

"Retaliation," Devin replies. "They've launched a nuclear weapon at San Diego."

"How long until impact?" Chris asks, solid.

"T-minus thirty-two minutes."

I cover my mouth with my hands.

That's not enough time to get out. That's just not enough.

Chris looks at me, all of the hope and love we shared just a moment ago dulled by the knowledge of our impending doom.

In just thirty-two minutes, we will be dead.

And our dreams will be dead with them.

Epilogue

Before the war, I loved very few people. Maybe no more than two.

There is just something about the battlefield that brings people together. Because when you're out there – and the bullets are flying and the fires are blazing – you're not just friends. You're brothers and sisters, bound by bloodshed and death and loyalty. I love so many people now. I love Chris, Uriah, Manny, Vera, Elle, Andrew and Arlene. They're not just my *people*, they're my family.

Nothing will take that away from me. I won't allow it.

There are so many questions that need to be answered. So many battles that have to be fought. Will we survive the next year? The next week? The next *day?*

It's so easy to live in fear, to be terrified of what Omega will do next.

But I will not be afraid anymore.

I will face the end with courage, with Chris by my side, and with my family around me.

Win or lose, live or die. We will give it everything we have.

We are the last fighters.

We are fear itself.

To Be Continued in

State of Allegiance

Book 9 of The Collapse Series

All Titles by Summer Lane

The Collapse Series

The Zero Trilogy

Graphic Guides

Collapse: The Illustrated Guide

The Bravo Saga

Bravo: Apocalypse Mission

Bravo: Blood Road

About the Author

Summer Lane is the #1
bestselling author of *The
Collapse Series, The Zero
Trilogy* and *The Bravo Saga.*
She is also the author of
*Collapse: The Illustrated
Guide*, a #1 bestselling
companion to her original
series.

Summer owns WB Publishing. She is an accomplished
journalist and creative writing teacher. She also owns
Writing Belle, an online magazine about the art of
storytelling, where she has interviewed and worked
with countless authors from around the globe.

Summer lives in the Central Valley of California, where
she enjoys reading, collecting tea, and visiting the beach
and mountains with her fiancé, Scott.

Connect with Summer Lane:

Twitter: @SummerEllenLane

Facebook: Summer Lane – Int. Bestselling Author

Website: summerlaneauthor.com

Blog: writingbelle.com

Email Summer with letters or thoughts about her books! She loves to hear from readers.

Email: summerlane101@gmail.com

Send her a letter:

Summer Lane/WB Publishing

P.O. Box 994

Reedley, CA 93654

Love Dogs?

Civilization, collapsed. Society, gone.

The apocalypse rules all, and mankind struggles for survival.

But there was a dog, and his name was Bravo.

**

Discover his story, a tale of bravery and adventure.

Pick up this thrilling, #1 bestselling phenomenon on Amazon
and Barnes & Noble from prolific author Summer Lane.

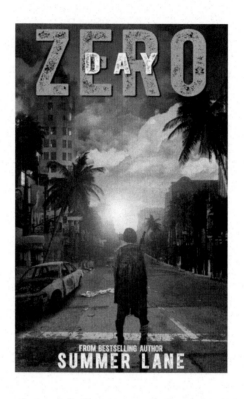

One girl. One sword. One dog.

Pick up the #1 Bestselling Zero Trilogy by

Summer Lane.

Featuring Bravo the bomb dog and Elle, the fearless,

teenage warrior of the apocalypse.

Available on Amazon and Barnes & Noble.

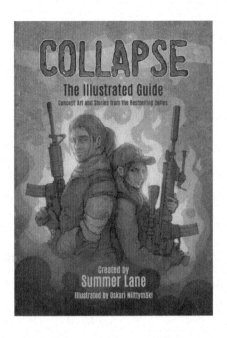

Collapse: The Illustrated Guide

Love Cassidy Hart? Love Elle?

Explore designs from 20 of the most popular characters from both series. Enjoy concept art and three exclusive short stories from Chris Young, Sophia Rodriguez and Harry Lydell.

Always available for just 99 cents on Amazon & Barnes & Noble.

Acknowledgements

I am not afraid to say that this book was a challenge! Of course, every book is a challenge, in some way, but this one was particularly interesting because of the new story aspects that Cassidy is now facing – from traveling to new places to finding herself submerged in the belly of a submarine. Suffice it to say that much research was done, and many days were spent in the office, poring over tons of information and trying to figure out what to call a siren on a sub. (The answer to that question is a klaxon!)

I would be remiss if I did not take a moment to thank everyone who helped this novel come to life. I run a tight ship (no submarine pun intended) here at WB Publishing, and this book seriously gave me a run for my money. The relief I feel at releasing it at last is palpable. I am even tempted to take a vacation.

I'd like to thank my fiancé, Scott, who was the award-worthy guy who encouraged me to utilize submarines in this novel like I've always wanted. If it wasn't for him, I don't know what I would have done! Good thing I'm marrying him this year, I need that kind of encouragement in my life. (insert mischievous wink here)

And then there is my brother, who was casually having a discussion about ice and caves and glaciers over a cup of tea in my office (let it be noted here that *I* was the one with the tea), which gave me the idea to take Cassidy to the Mendenhall Glacier. Thanks for the inspiration, bro!

Thanks to Don for going through the novel. Yes, I'm an adult, but I still like getting my Daddy's opinion on my books to this day! It's just one of those things. Thanks for working with my crazy, crazy schedule, Jake – your editing is helpful. Flexibility is the cardinal sign of a snazzy individual. You're pretty snazzy! The same goes for Giselle – another flexible cool cat. I'm lucky to work with people like you.

Thanks to the forty-six sub-readers and beta commentators that helped make this book even better than I thought it could possibly be! Also, a special shout-out to Steven for again making a great cover for my book. I chose to highlight the Roamers' fortress for the cover because I thought it was something that we haven't seen before. It took some tweaking to get it right, but we pulled through!

This book is a fast-paced action novel that finally gets to some of the emotional moments that I've been positively dying to flesh out (especially between Chris and Cassidy!).

State of Fear is, simply put, the prologue to the final two installments of the series, which will be longer and more detailed than any of the installments before it. I promise a slam-bang finish for you guys with the last two books, *State of Allegiance* and *State of Hope*. It's important to me to create an ending for the series that will be worthy of the characters who have become my dear friends – and yours, too.

I'll be working on these books over the next year and a half. So don't worry. There's still time to theorize about what's going to happen next!

As a final note, I think it's interestingly ironic that in the same book that Cassidy has finally reached a state of engagement (Ha. Ha.) with Chris, that I am getting married. I have talked about this a lot on my website and in interviews, but I can't get over this coincidence. I honestly did not plan it out this way – it just happened!

Thanks for being such awesome readers, and for carrying Cassidy all around the world. Here's to the next 100,000 readers!